SASSY BLONDE

USA TODAY BESTSELLING AUTHOR

STACEY KENNEDY

For all the dreamers

Stacey Kennedy

www.staceykennedy.com

Edited by Lexi Smail

Copy Edited by Jolene Perry

Proofread by Christa Désir

Cover Design by Regina Wamba

Manufactured in Canada

PROLOGUE

Maisie Carter followed her two older sisters, Clara and Amelia, out of the big, white, colonial-style house, the gravel driveway crunching under her pink Converse, and the blistering hot sun above promising a beautiful day. Clara was all the things Maisie wasn't. Responsible. Organized. Dependable. Not that Maisie didn't try to be those things, but she always came up short. Amelia's personality had always fallen smack dab between Clara's buttoned-up ways and Maisie's free spirit. Amelia was definitely the most well-adjusted.

Maisie stayed a step behind as they headed toward the black barn that once belonged to their beloved grandfather, Pops. He'd passed away a month ago, leaving the farm, an idea for a brewery, and all his savings to the three sisters. A blessing, for sure, and not an unexpected one either. Their grandfather had raised them after their parents died in a fiery car crash. Maisie had only been four months old. Amelia was two, and Clara four. None of them remembered their parents, and maybe that was a good thing. The loss didn't feel so great, not when they'd been raised by their father's doting parents. A heart attack had stolen their grandmother away five years go. And a month ago, Pops had gone too.

Maisie missed her grandparents. Even now, when Pops's last wish had created a dark cloud over Maisie's life. She was an artist and never wanted to own a brewery, but she'd always kept that thought to herself.

Hindsight was a bitch.

"How long until the beer is ready?" Clara, their oldest sister, asked Amelia. Clara had long, reddish-brown hair that she wore in a tight ponytail most days, and a good three inches of height on Maisie. She was pretty in a very elegant way. Her fine features and full lips belonged on an old Hollywood movie screen.

Next to her, Amelia answered, "Weeks away still. I'm close to getting the formula right, but something is still missing." The sunlight picked up the natural golden highlights in Amelia's hair. At twenty-six years old, and with her ginger-colored hair and freckles dusting her nose, Maisie would argue that Amelia was the prettiest sister.

Both her sisters took after their mother with the reddish hue in their hair. Maisie didn't have a drop of red in her blond hair. Even physically, she was their opposite, the outcast, the one in the family who didn't actually belong. Clara and Amelia had always been cut from the same cloth. Maisie had always been...*different.* Even now, as she walked behind them while they planned the future of their craft brewery, she knew that while she owned one-third of the business, no one really expected her to put much into the company...besides designing the logo. Which she'd done as soon as they'd come up with the name: Three Chicks Brewery. Pops had always called them *the three chicklets*, a spin-off from the Three Musketeers. The name felt right, and she used the old *Charlie's Angels* logo as inspiration for the design, drawing her and her sisters each holding a beer bottle, with the name in calligraphy. But this company belonged to Clara and Amelia, and everyone knew it.

The business plan was simple: Clara, with her business degree, would handle all of the logistics of running the brewery. Amelia had become a brewmaster last year after finishing a program in Denver and was adjusting their grandfather's homemade brew for market to a larger audience. And Maisie...well, she was the third wheel, the one who had a stake in the business, but was completely and totally out of her league.

When they entered the barn, Maisie followed, greeted by cobwebs, an old straw floor, and a moldy scent mixed with thick dust. A loud war scream echoed in the barn, and a blur of light brown hair and bright green eyes rushed by.

Clara's four-year-old son, Mason, charged forward, a fake sword in his hands, while he ran to hunt and kill the monsters in the barn.

"Please don't hurt yourself, buddy," Clara called to him before she addressed Amelia again. "I've got the construction crew coming out tomorrow to begin demolition."

Maisie laughed as Mason attacked a wooden beam like a fierce warrior. Her nephew had two speeds—super and torpedo. He never sat down. Ever. Maisie stayed by the open double doors, leaning against the frame, having nothing to add. She didn't know a thing about running a brewery. She knew how to mix colors to create perfect hues. How to use a pencil shading to bring a drawing to life. How to see beauty and replicate it. Before Pops passed away, she'd *just* finished her art major. In fact, she'd been days away from asking Clara to go into business with her. Maisie wanted to open her own art studio, selling her art and teaching children and adults how to draw. She wanted to host paint nights. She wanted to inspire people to dream, to create, to live their passion. But then Pops died, leaving them the property, along with a letter indicating he wanted them to use the money to open a brewery like he and her sisters had always talked about. He also left a personal letter to each of them.

Only problem, Pops didn't know that Maisie didn't want anything to do with the brewery. She had her own dreams.

"You look miserable."

Maisie smiled and turned to find her favorite person in the world, Laurel Taylor, her best friend since the first grade. Laurel was a little taller than Maisie and had honey-blond hair that reached the middle of her back, but it was her soft green eyes that welcomed a person in. She had the kindest eyes Maisie had ever seen. So full of love. Maisie hugged Laurel tight before she said, "I didn't know you were coming by."

Laurel gestured over her shoulder. "We were visiting Hayes's dad, so I wanted to stop by before we head back home. Just missing you."

Maisie hugged her again. Even tighter. "I'm missing you too." She noted Hayes sitting in the driver's seat of his black car. Hayes had whiskey-colored eyes and was a rough-around-the-edges kind of man, with slightly wavy choco-late-brown hair that was cut short on the sides and longer on top. Laurel and Hayes had been together since Laurel was eighteen. Back then, it had been a bit of a scandal since Hayes was twenty-four. But everyone saw how in love they were, and even their parents finally got over the big age gap. Maisie had always been happy for them, until Hayes received a job offer from the Denver Police Department and they moved away from their hometown of River Rock.

Maisie waved, and Hayes waved back as Laurel asked,

"When are you going to tell them you don't want to do this?"

Maisie cringed. "How about never?"

Laurel frowned, crossing her arms over her mauve tank top. She glanced into the barn, obviously making sure Clara and Amelia couldn't hear her before she said, "You need to be honest with your sisters. Everything is in the planning stages right now. Tell them you want your cut of what your grandfather left to open the art studio like we talked about. I'll buy that quaint coffee shop right next door and drive from Denver every day. We'll finally see our dreams come true." Those had been their dream jobs since they were in the seventh grade. Their plan.

Maisie's heart hurt. "I can't pull out money from the brewery before they even get it going. Pops left everything so this dream could happen for them. What kind of horrible person would I be if I went back on his wishes?"

Laurel unlocked her arms and took Maisie's hand. "Okay, that's fair, but ask yourself this: Would Pops have left all this money for the brewery if he knew your heart wasn't really in it?"

"Probably not," Maisie said. He would have ensured Maisie fought for her dreams too.

Laurel gave a firm nod of agreement. "All I'm saying is, your sisters have their dreams. They've always been close like that. Made plans together. Done *everything* together, like *we* do everything together. But don't forget about you and your dreams."

Maisie threw her arms around Laurel, always feeling like Laurel understood her when no one else did. "You always fight for the best for me. Thank you for that."

Laurel squeezed back tight, resting her head on Maisie's shoulder. "You don't need to thank me, babe. I love you like crazy, and you'd be saying the same thing to me."

"I love you too," Maisie whispered.

Those words echoed in the air for a moment, and suddenly, the warmth seeping from Laurel's hold began to vanish...replaced by something dark...something cold.

She blinked, realizing she was not standing outside with Laurel anymore. She tried to remember how she got back inside her house but failed miserably. Hayes was not sitting in his car waiting for her best friend to return to him. Laurel's soft voice, her smile...*gone*. The sun had disappeared, bringing a dark, eerie night. Maisie pressed her hands flat against the cool hardwood floor in the foyer of the house, barely able to drag in breaths. Screams blasted against the walls, until she realized the sounds of pure agony came from her mouth. Her pile of vomit lay next to her, some soaking her nightgown.

She'd *just* been with Laurel today. They had *just* talked. *Just* hugged.

Maisie forced her gaze up. Hayes stared down at her, his expression unreadable, his whiskey-colored eyes were dead...*empty*. His mouth was moving, but the screams from her mouth wouldn't stop, the roaring in her ears too loud.

Hands suddenly grabbed her, and Maisie had enough sense to recognize it was her sisters, dragging her away from her vomit.

People began yelling, panic and confusion ripping through the house. Mason stood on the staircase sobbing before Clara ran to him, her nightgown fluttering with the movement.

Time no longer existed, not for Maisie, as Hayes turned and strode out of the house, leaving the front door wide open. He became a blur of navy that faded into the night. Only then did she fully process what he had said.

"Murder. Robbery gone wrong. Laurel...she's gone."

1

TWO YEARS LATER...

Maisie's paintbrush swept across the canvas, mixing the darker green paint in with the lighter, creating depth to the trees of the forest. The sun's beams warmed her face, the wind swishing the long grasses behind her, while her painting of the sweeping meadow flowed easily. "Not Picasso yet," she noted, leaning back to admire her work. She caught a hundred things wrong with the painting, but nothing that couldn't be fixed at home. Few things made her feel content, but replicating the beauty in the world was one of them.

The slight heaviness in her eyelids from waking up at the crack of dawn was worth the spike of happiness painting gave her. She wiped off her paintbrush, tucking her supplies into her tote bag with COOL AF ARTIST written on the side, a present from her sisters for her birthday last year. The last letter from her grandfather peeked out from the bag. She reached for it as she heard the flapping of wings overhead. She unfolded the piece of paper and revealed the quote by Michelangelo: *The greatest danger for most of us is*

not that our aim is too high and we miss it, but that it is too low
and we reach it.

Even after two years, Maisie still didn't know what Pops meant by this or why he'd chosen this quote as his very last thing to say to her. She'd never asked what Pops wrote in her sisters' letters, and neither Clara nor Amelia had offered the information up.

Thinking of her sisters, and knowing she had a mile-long to-do list today, Maisie checked the time on her phone that rested on a fallen log next to her.

"Shit!" She jolted up, grabbed her bag and canvas, and took off running. The alarm she'd set to remind her about work hadn't gone off. Her footsteps were muffled in the grass, but a squirrel ran away from her as she charged up the small hill. When she reached the top, she spotted the long driveway that led to the house and the black barn—now turned into a brewery—off to the right of it.

Prepared for a lecture, Maisie stopped at her MINI Cooper and deposited her tote bag and canvas onto the passenger seat before she hurried into the barn. Rows of huge steel tanks filled the space, with a main walkway that led to a room in the back for tastings. Some days the brewery held a metallic scent. Other days, it smelled earthy. As Maisie sucked in a breath, she realized today, it smelled fruity.

As she made her way through the tanks, she caught sight of Amelia, bent over the rim of a tank. Maisie held her breath and tiptoed past. Amelia must have been brewing last night and was now cleaning out the tank. She'd gotten into the habit of brewing Foxy Diva—their top-selling beer that had won over the locals—at night, since the brewery was part of local tours for travelers during the day.

"I see you," Amelia called.

Maisie stopped dead and said in a ghostly voice, "I'm a figment of your imagination."

Amelia laughed, straightening up. She had grain covering her ugly yellow apron with matching latex gloves. "Nice try," she said, wiping the sweat beading on her forehead with her covered arm. "You better hurry before Clara sees you're late. Again."

"What do you mean, late?" Maisie asked, fluttering her lashes. "I've been here for an hour already. You need sleep, Amelia. Seriously, you need to take better care of yourself." Before Amelia could respond, Maisie booked it, walking faster now. Clara only understood punctual. Maisie missed that gene.

"Hey, Maisie," Amelia called, just as Maisie reached the door to storage room. "You've got paint on your cheek."

Dammit. Maisie went to swipe away the paint when she walked straight into something hard. She bounced back and glanced up into something harder. Clara's stormy blue eyes. "Hi," Maisie said with a tight smile. "Oh, you look so pretty today."

Not falling for it, Clara frowned, crossing her arms over her lacy blouse. "Three festivals. That's what you've got on your plate for this week."

Maisie nodded. "Yup. Got it."

She slinked away when Clara's cold voice stopped her. "You know what these festivals mean for us? This is our chance to take Foxy Diva and actually make something happen. If we screw this up, we need to start all over. You get that, right?"

Again, Maisie nodded. "Yes, I know how important the festivals are. Don't you worry one bit. Everyone will know Foxy Diva's name by the time I'm done with the festivals." It took two years for Amelia to perfect their grandfather's homemade brew. Maisie had come up with the name and the logo, which at least fed Maisie's creative side, but now, she was expected to go on a road trip through Colorado to give their beer exposure. "I've got this handled. Promise. And I'm sorry I was late."

Clara swiped at Maisie's cheek, pulling away with a green finger. "You were painting again."

It wasn't a question. "A little, but the sunrise today was absolutely gorgeous. Besides, blame this one on my phone. I set my alarm to get here on time, but it didn't go off. This time, it's not my fault."

Clara softened a smidgen. Like, a miniscule. "I don't mean to be hard on you, but we can't make mistakes now. You two put me in charge of running this company, so you have to trust me to do that, and take my advice seriously. We need to make sure we stand out at these festivals to get a buzz going. Without that, Foxy Diva cannot and will not take off." Which was the only thing anyone thought about lately.

To be successful, Foxy Diva needed to become a staple across North America. So far, locally, they'd made it a huge success, but they needed distribution across North America to actually make decent money. They wanted Foxy Diva to be in every restaurant. Every bar. Every beer store. Or at least, Clara and Amelia did, and Maisie just followed along, doing her part to make the beer a hit.

Clara uncrossed her arms to take Maisie by the shoulders. She dropped her gaze to Maisie's eye level. "I'm going to ask you again: Are you sure you can do this? No one is going to fault you if this is too much."

Maisie could barely hold Clara's fierce stare. Part of her wanted to run and hide, mortified her sisters were gliding through this brewery gig, while Maisie was basically drowning. She was an artist, not a business-minded person. But she owed this to Pops. He'd left them everything to make this dream happen. His final wish. And heck, she'd bartended for years. "It's not too hard. I've got this. One hundred percent. You don't need to worry."

The look Clara gave her said she didn't believe her. Though blessedly, she let Maisie off the hook and changed the subject. "I need to go to the post office. I've got Foxy Diva entered into five more contests, so I need to mail in the samples." Which was how beer contests happened. Now all they had to do was wait to see if Foxy Diva won any awards.

"That's great news," Amelia cut in. "I'm crossing my fingers something comes of the awards. That will help us nail a distributor more than anything else."

Maisie rolled her eyes. "Oh, sure, now you're part of the conversation." What about helping her out when Clara cornered her?

Amelia shrugged. "Just 'cause I'm the middle sister doesn't mean I need to get in the middle of everything, including your conversations." To Clara, she asked, "How long do you think it'll take before we get the results?"

"Months," Clara said with a long sigh before her voice perked back up. "But getting the awards is really just step one. We need to get buzz going, and social media is our greatest tool for that."

"Which is where I come in?" Maisie asked.

"Exactly." Clara nodded. "When we finally go to the distributor, we need all the ammunition to stand out from the other hundreds of craft beers sent their way."

"And," Amelia added, "if we get enough buzz going, they might come to us."

Great. If that wasn't a reason to drink, Maisie didn't know what was. To avoid the pressure that became near suffocating, she grabbed the door handle to the storage room. "Well, I've got a four-day road trip, and a trailer that isn't going to pack itself. See you later."

"Maisie." At Clara's soft voice, Maisie froze. "I know today has to be hard for you. Are you okay?"

Maisie shut her eyes and breathed deep. She'd avoided thinking about what today was ever since she'd woken up. It was why she'd gone and painted, to bring a little brightness to a very dark day. But there was no running away. The articles that splashed across the media two years ago haunted her: *Murder Rattles the Small Town of River Rock. Young Woman Brutally Murdered. Officer Hayes Taylor Leaves Denver Police Department After Wife's Murder.*

Laurel's murder had been declared a robbery gone wrong at their home in Denver. Hayes had hunted down her killer, and after a shoot-out, the killer was dead. After that, he quit his job and moved back home to River Rock. But even with the justice of finding Laurel's murderer, nothing had been the same since. For a month, Maisie could barely breathe, function. Her sisters had come to her aid. They'd fed her, forced her to shower, brought her out of the darkest place Maisie had ever gone. Laurel's absence felt like half of Maisie's body was missing, and she'd struggled to learn how to walk again. But slowly, through her sisters' love, things had gotten better, and Maisie remembered how to take one step in front of the other. More importantly, she remembered life was a one-time deal. The loss of her parents, of Pops, and of Laurel had taught her that. The world, her life, was far too beautiful and special to waste the time she had.

For Laurel, for her parents, and for her grandparents, she looked for the beauty every day, until the beauty was all she saw. She drew and painted and never stopped until that ache in her chest, while still there, didn't shadow her happiness.

"I'm okay," she told her sisters, glancing back at them with the smile she knew they needed to see. "Thanks for worrying about me, but really, I'm remembering the good stuff about Laurel, not the bad memory that took her away. I know she'd want that."

Amelia gave a gentle smile. "You're right, she would."

Clara added, "We're here for you."

Maisie glanced between her sisters. She'd always felt so different from them growing up, but Laurel's death had changed that. And the best friend that gave so much love to Maisie, in death, had brought Maisie closer to her sisters. They'd loved her hard through her grief and brought her back from that unforgiving pain. For that, Maisie had stuffed her dreams of owning an art studio far away, giving all of herself to the brewery, even if she was late and didn't always get things right. "Thanks," she said to her sisters. "Now let me get back to work, would ya? Geesh, you're always holding me up. Don't you know I have a thousand things to do today?"

Amelia laughed softly.

Clara rolled her eyes.

Maisie chuckled, reminding herself that laughing was good. Especially on days like today. Smiling, enjoying life, was the best way she could honor Laurel's life. She finally pulled the heavy door open and hurried through, when the reality of what was ahead of her hit her like a brick to the face. The first festival was in Fort Collins, then Colorado Springs, finishing up in Boulder. Panic creeped up like icy fingertips along her spine. She was in way over her head, never having done anything like this before. Her pink Converse scraped against the rough floor as she moved farther into the storage room, her nose scrunching at the musty air.

Pushing aside her fear of failing—since failure was not an option—she pulled out the note in her back pocket of her blue jeans, scribbled with her to-do list. The first item on that list: *kegs.* She grabbed the dolly, moving toward the kegs with the Foxy Diva label. She smiled at the label of the vintage sexy pin-up woman with *Foxy Diva* written in calligraphy around her. Maisie was proud of the design, and she was still surprised Clara approved the logo. But Foxy Diva was an Indian pale ale with a buttload of spices that Maisie knew nothing about, and Amelia had said the spiciness of the woman fit the beer inside perfectly. That had been the first time Amelia had ever taken Maisie's side, and Maisie still felt the high from that.

Determined to get the trailer packed and the workday behind her, Maisie shoved the dolly under the keg and pulled back, her arms shaking as the dolly caught the edge of the keg.

She wobbled once.

And again.

Then she was falling. And something metal and shiny and *big* was coming with her.

Hayes Taylor refused to acknowledge today's anniversary and kept his focus on this work, like he'd done every day for the last two years. The past was behind him, and he stood firmly in the present at Blackshaw Training, a horse training facility. Over the past sixteen months he'd worked there, he had seen a dangerous horse now and again, but nothing like the chestnut gelding with the white stripe currently staring him down. *Threat*. The gelding's black eyes screamed at Hayes. *Danger*. And at the particular moment, Hayes was dangerous to the gelding. Horsemanship wasn't about breaking an animal. It was about communicating, and somewhere in this horse's life, that communication crossed a line it shouldn't have.

"First thoughts?" Hayes asked, turning to Beckett Stone, his good friend since high school. Beckett's sandy-brown hair didn't seem to have a style, and his face needed a good shave. But Beckett's rough edge was what the ladies liked most. Or so the gossip around town suggested.

Beckett removed his Stetson and ran a hand through his hair. "I think you've got your hands full with that one. And if it were me, I'd be wearing full body gear anytime I was near him."

Hayes snorted, hooking his boot up on the fence railing. "That's why you don't ride the troubled ones and instead handle the young ones."

Unbothered by the remark, Beckett barked a laugh. "Yeah, 'cause I'm not looking to die at thirty."

While they were the same age, and Beckett hadn't meant the remark as a dig, two years ago, Hayes *was* looking for that. Even he could admit that he'd taken risks a sane man wouldn't. He gravitated toward working with mentally broken horses because he felt equally broken himself. He hadn't recovered from Laurel's death. When his wife was murdered, Hayes lost it. As a cop, he should have stopped it. After Laurel's murder, he couldn't protect anyone anymore. He walked away from the badge and his job at the Denver Police Department, moved back to River Rock, and found a home at Blackshaw Training. Getting back to a simpler life had been his salvation.

Hayes took a deep breath, letting go of the tension rising

in his chest. The west wind picked up the floral scents of wildflower and ringing wind chimes in the distance. Hayes glanced back at the two-story log house with the wide, covered deck where Nash Blackshaw, the owner of the farm, lived with his wife, Megan, and son. A black-roofed barn housed injured horses or horses needing stabling for the night. Next to the barn was the sand ring used for training. Every sound, from the hooves stomping the ground, to tails swooshing, to the horses whinnying, all brought Hayes back to a place before Laurel's murder. His childhood. He'd grown up working on the Blackshaws' cattle farm during his summers throughout high school and police training. Those years held some of his favorite memories. His happiest for sure, when things with Laurel had been quiet and good, and she'd come out to the farm to go on a ride.

"Let me see exactly what his owners want from us," Hayes finally said to Beckett.

Beckett slid his hat back in place. "Good luck. Remember not to sign your death warrant. You are allowed to turn down a job."

Hayes nodded but didn't reply. Saying no was near impossible after one look at the heartbroken teenage girl who came out of the barn to meet them. She wore fancy equestrian gear, beige breeches, tall, shiny black boots, and a black T-shirt. Her long blond hair was pulled up in a tight ponytail and her makeup was heavy. Hayes entered the ring, moving toward the horse that kept a close eye on him.

Colin Calloway, the father of the teenage girl, approached. He wore a suit, looked fancy, and he'd paid a good chunk of cash for a horse who was trained in show jumping and suddenly decided it didn't want to do its job anymore.

"What did you see?" the father asked when he reached

Hayes.

"A dangerous horse," Hayes stated simply.

Colin's dark eyebrows went up. "You got that from one look?"

"I got that from the way he's sizing me up."

Colin sighed and glanced back at his daughter, who had walked up to the horse and stroked his face. "Every trainer I've taken him to doesn't know what's wrong with him. It's like a switch goes off. One second, he's approachable. The next, the devil gets into him."

Hayes started to explain that the problem wasn't the horse, but the communication between the horse and the human, when suddenly Hayes caught the pinning of the horse's ears, the tensing of his muscles. He jolted forward in the same second the horse went in for a bite. Hayes none-too-gently shoved the teenager aside, sending her toppling over, and rammed himself into the horse, getting his attention off the girl.

The gelding's head shot up and his nostrils flared as he flew backward. Hayes grabbed the lead line, noting the girl getting up and out of the way. He acted immediately, using the end of the lead line to circle in the air and make the horse's feet move. Hayes moved hard, fast, not stopping, until the only thing the horse was looking at was him. Without glancing behind him, he led the gelding to one of the individual paddocks, away from the other horses, and closed the gate. He took a few steps back, ensuring the horse didn't ram the gate, then turned back, finding the girl brushing the sand off her pants. "I'm sorry about that. Are you okay?"

"Don't apologize," the father said firmly, offering his hand. "You saved her from an injury, but now, you can see what we're dealing with."

Hayes returned the shake and then moved closer to the girl, noting her curled shoulders. "You're all right?" he repeated.

She lifted her head. Her smile looked forced. "Yes, I'm okay. Thank you."

He got that pain in her eyes. Pain that came from a situation where a person had no control. "We'll get him right for you. Don't worry about that. Okay?"

Her chin quivered and her green eyes welled with tears. "Was it me that did this? I...I just keep thinking maybe I worked him too hard or something."

Hayes dropped a hand on her shoulder and brought his gaze down to hers. "Nothin' you've done caused this. The wires in his head aren't firing right. We'll get him straightened out."

"Yeah?" she barely managed.

He gave her the firm nod she needed. "Without a doubt."

This time when she smiled, there was warmth there. "Thank you."

"Any idea how long it will take?" Colin asked.

Hayes tucked his hands into his pockets and shrugged. "The gelding decides that."

They both seemed all right with that answer and confident in him, since they left a few minutes later, with Hayes's promise of a daily email updating them on the progress. Hayes grabbed a few flakes of hay from the barn and the sweet scent infused the air as he tossed the flakes into the gelding's paddock. He rubbed the fallen strands off his T-shirt when his cell phone rang. He smiled when he saw the name on the screen. "What trouble are you in now?"

A pause. "How do you know I'm in trouble?" Maisie asked.

Laurel and Maisie had been the best of friends since

elementary school. Not bound by blood, but what they held had been deeper. And Maisie had been that type of friend to Hayes ever since Laurel's death. "Because it's midmorning and you never call me midmorning."

A beat passed. The horse came over and began eating the hay.

Maisie finally spoke, her voice tight. "Fine. You're right. I'm stuck under a keg and need your help."

Hayes leaned his arm against the top of the coarse wooded fence. "Say that again?" He had to have heard her wrong.

She sighed heavily. "Please don't make me repeat it."

He grinned. "Sorry, I'm going to need you to."

Another sigh, even more exaggerated this time. "I'm stuck under a beer keg in the storage area and need you to come help me."

Unsure if this was serious or not, since on any given day, Maisie always seemed to get herself in unusual situations, he decided not to drag this along. "I'll be there in ten."

"Thank you. Oh, and Hayes?"

"Yeah?"

"Please don't say anything about this to Clara or Amelia."

Hayes chuckled. "Mum's the word." He ended the call and approached his black RAM truck.

Maisie was the most accident-prone person he'd ever met. If something went wrong, she was usually involved. Hayes had tried to distance himself from Maisie after Laurel's funeral. Hell, he'd tried to distance himself from everyone. Only Maisie and Beckett hadn't allowed it. Hayes was pretty sure he'd be lost or dead without them.

The drive to the brewery took him eight minutes, and when he reached the farm, he drove up the long driveway, pulling in next to Maisie's MINI. A beautiful landscape painting sat on the passenger seat. Maisie had more natural talent than Hayes had ever seen. He, for one, thought she wasted it working in a brewery, but who was he to argue with her life choices? He certainly had no idea where his life was headed anymore.

When he entered through the side door, he caught Amelia's curses. She was bent over in the tank, looking like she belonged in a chemical lab. "What's the brew this time?" he asked.

Amelia jerked up in surprise, covered in spent grain. She smiled when she realized who stood before her. "It's a fruity beer I'm playing around with. You'd hate it."

"Then I won't ask for sample," he said. Playing cool, he asked, "I'm here to see Maisie. She in the back?"

Amelia wiped the sweat off her forehead with her arm. "Yeah, she's getting ready for some festivals."

"Nice." He gave an easy smile, hoping to hell Amelia didn't pick up on his urgency, and gestured at the tanks. "Hope your day gets better."

"You and me both." She laughed.

Hayes loosed the breath he didn't know he was holding as he left her behind. Luckily, Clara wasn't in her office when he strode by. She was the toughest sister, and he really didn't want to lie to her. When he passed the last rows of tanks, he lengthened his stride. The second he walked into the open storage area, he called, "Maisie."

"Shh," she said to his right. "Close the door."

He shut the door gently and followed her voice, stopping short when he saw her. He didn't initially see the problem. She was lying on her back, like she was waiting for *him*. His body temperature rose, his groin filling with heat. That wildly inappropriate reaction to her had started happening a few months ago. It was the day he remembered he was a man. Maisie had come to see him at the farm and wore a sexy, short dress. The hard-on that followed, and every single one after it when she came near him, told him how truly fucked up he was. She was his friend, not his to lust over. But when he finally spotted her hand stuck under a keg, he rushed forward. "Shit, Maisie. What happened?"

She gave him a lopsided smile. "I tried to move the keg. It didn't like that."

He circled her, getting a good look at the keg. "How hurt is your hand?"

"It's fine," she said. "Not hurting one bit. Get this off me."

He doubted she wasn't hurt but settled in front of the keg to free her. "I think there's only one thing to say now."

"What's that?"

He grabbed the top handle of the keg. "This might sting a little." As fast as he could, he yanked the keg up until she could pull her arm out.

Her eyes shut, lips parted in a silent scream, and her skin lost all of its color. "I'm okay," she gasped, breathing deep. "I'm okay."

He set the keg down and took one look at her hand. "Hate to break it to you, Maisie, but you're definitely not okay."

She slowly opened her eyes and looked at her finger that was bent in the wrong direction. Her eyes flicked to his and became distant. "Uh-oh." Then she cried out in pain, those same eyes rolling into the back of her head.

He dropped to his knees, placing a hand on her head.

The door whisked open and Amelia rushed in, breathless. "Oh my God, what's wrong?"

"It's safe to say that no matter how bad you think your day is, Maisie's is worse."

2

"You're fired."

Maisie balked at Clara, trying to ignore the dinging alarm coming from the hospital room across the hallway. She'd been in the hospital for six terribly long hours now. After she'd been knocked out, and an orthopedic surgeon realigned the fracture fragments, they'd given her a horribly ugly splint. While that all sucked, the worst part was that she had hurt her dominant hand. No painting. No drawing. No creating. For...weeks? That was bad. But this? "You can't fire me," she implored.

"You and Amelia gave me full control of running the business, so I obviously can," Clara said, placing her hands on her hips. "Even before your accident, I seriously doubted you could do this. Now? Maisie, let's be real here, you can't handle the festivals."

Defeat sank in, and even Maisie doubted herself, but yet, she still asked, "Who says I can't?"

Clara waved at the saline bag attached to Maisie's hand and then pointed at Maisie's broken finger. "I'd say today is evidence enough this isn't working out." Her sister's expression softened, and she took Maisie's uninjured hand and squeezed tight. "I know you wanted to do something more for the brewery than the logos and signage, and you tried. We're proud of you."

Amelia nodded and gave a soft smile. "So proud."

Clara added, "But you've been struggling at this before you even hit the ground running. We'll just have to find you something else to do within the company."

But there wasn't anything else for Maisie to do, and they all knew it. Clara was the brains of the operation. Amelia was creator of the beer. Even, Penelope, their cousin, had taken over the brewery tours since Maisie, well...sucked at that too. Maisie was the painter, the dreamer, the woman trying desperately to fit into the box that she didn't fit in. "Okay, I know having the keg fall on my hand wasn't my finest moment," she hedged, "but I can fix this."

Clara's brows rose. "How?"

"I'll figure that out soon," Maisie said with a smile.

Clara frowned. "That sugary sweet smile has gotten you many, *many* chances, but I'm afraid you're out of them."

No! No. This couldn't happen. Clara and Amelia had been fulfilling their end of their bargain. Maisie may have broken her finger, but she was determined to do the same. To help fulfill Pops's final wish. "Just give me one more try," she pleaded. "Please."

Obviously taking pity on Maisie, Amelia cut in, nudging Clara's arm. "It's not going to hurt anyone to give her one more chance."

A muscle near Clara's eye twitched. Like, maybe a few of those gray hairs she dyed lately were because of Maisie. She finally huffed, then said to Maisie, "I don't even pretend to know how you'll pull this off, but fine, one more chance.

That's it, though, Maisie. Our reputation is riding on these festivals."

"Got it," Maisie said with a firm nod.

Clara loosed another breath and stepped closer to the bed to drop a kiss on Maisie's forehead. "I'm sorry about your finger."

Clara wasn't all tough. She had an incredibly soft heart. It was just that her heart had thorns around it, ready to hurt, if need be. Maisie couldn't blame her. Clara had Mason to think of, and being a single mom was a big weight. The brewery had to succeed.

"Thanks," Maisie said, studying her finger in the splint. "It actually doesn't even hurt anymore." She smiled at her sisters. "But maybe that's the morphine talking."

Amelia chuckled, her eyes twinkling. "Probably, but since you are feeling better, how about I go see about getting you out of here?"

"Lord, yes, please." Maisie had been stuffed into a semi-private room, the blue curtain separating her and the next bed. She didn't want to be there when that next person came in.

Clara grabbed her purse off the seat. "I need to pick up Mason from the sitter. She's probably wondering where I am." When Clara reached the curtain, she turned back. "You're really okay?"

Maisie nodded. "The only thing hurting right now is my ego."

Clara's brow wrinkled, obviously disbelieving. "Okay, call me if you need me. I'll stop off at the pharmacy and pick up your painkiller prescription"

Maisie often felt bad for Clara. The burden of responsibility always rested on her shoulders. Maisie couldn't remember the last time Clara ever did anything for herself.

"Thanks. Love you." She forced a smile, giving her sisters a quick wave before they shut the curtain closed behind them.

The moment they were gone, tears pricked Maisie's eyelids. One more chance, and then what? Before she broke her finger, she had doubts she could pull off the beer festivals without epically screwing up. Now? Even she knew the finish line was near impossible to reach. She couldn't even move a damn keg without it falling on her.

This was beginning to feel like a nightmare she couldn't wake up from. Being a disappointment to her sisters was normal. She'd always been Maisie, the baby who always got caught sneaking out and never followed the rules. But disappointing her grandfather, not seeing his final wish for the girls he'd raised come true, was harder to stomach. She slowly breathed through the pain, knowing one thing for certain—she could not fail.

Voices stirred next to her as nurses rolled a bed in. A moment later, a high feminine voice snapped, "Sir, you need to stay in your bed."

"I'm fine. If you'd just let me go, I'd show you."

There was a muffled creak as the person adjusted in the bed before the nurse practically growled, "I'm going to sedate you if you don't stay put."

Maisie fought her laughter at that low baritone voice. Only one man would cause someone so much grief. She slid off the bed, grabbed the curtain, and whisked it open. First, she met the nurse's scowl. Then she met Hayes's whiskey-colored eyes. He practically filled the hospital bed with six-foot-two feet of pure, hardworking muscle. And just the sight of him warmed Maisie's belly.

That was a problem lately. Hayes had always been Laurel's guy. Then Hayes had become a friend. But over the last few months, something had shifted between them, and

Maisie still couldn't figure out why her heart suddenly wanted him. But there was no denying the draw there, the want, the *need*. She'd tried to fight her growing attraction, feeling horribly guilty, but there was no point. Her heart demanded Hayes. While she knew Laurel would want them to be happy, Hayes hadn't acted on the attraction, and neither had Maisie. *Yet.* To keep things light, she joked, "Aw, you felt so bad I was in here, you wanted to join me."

Hayes's mouth twitched, his eyes warming when they met hers. "Didn't want you feeling left out," he said.

A snort came from the doorway. Maisie glanced up, catching Beckett's bemused expression. "I told him to wear armor. He didn't listen."

Maisie smiled at Beckett, but her smile fell when she glanced at Hayes. "What happened?"

Hayes looked more than annoyed, his eye twitching. "After your sisters brought you here, I went back to the farm. I had little a disagreement with a horse."

"No," the nurse said. "He fell off a horse, and that's why he needs to stay in this bed."

Maisie gave Hayes a totally fake chastising look. "You're not being a terrible patient, are you?"

Hayes set his jaw. "I don't want to be a patient at all."

The nurse frowned at him. "You might have a concussion. The doctor wants you to stay overnight, just to be safe."

"Yeah, that's not happening." Hayes sat up, his large frame filling up the small space. He swung his legs over the side of the bed, sand falling off his cowboy boots.

Maisie took in the dirt covering his worn blue jeans and black T-shirt, realizing he most definitely did have a fall.

When he went to stand, she grabbed him by the arm with her uninjured hand, desperately aware of the muscles stretching and flexing beneath her fingers. "Don't be stupid." She pressed her hand to his chest and he willingly let her push him back on the bed. When the warmth of his eyes returned to hers, time stopped. She became instantly lost, trapped by the intensity she saw on his face. He slowly wrapped his fingers around her wrist, and maybe because it was the anniversary of Laurel's death, or something else altogether, but she remembered the last time his fingers wrapped around her wrist.

"Maisie. Go home."

Maisie stood in the dark bedroom in the empty house. She had no idea how bad Hayes's depression had gotten, when she'd been so deep in her own. Then Beckett called and begged her to help. Now, here, with Hayes, she couldn't believe her eyes, and yet, she understood, having been so lost herself.

The beautiful, expensive property that Hayes bought when he moved back to River Rock had been gorgeous when she'd come for the spreading of Laurel's ashes on the weeping willow hanging over the creek. Now, without him mowing the lawn or tending to the property, everything was overgrown. The three-bedroom house had no furniture. Hayes slept on a camping mat on the floor, the curtains on the windows were drawn. The darkness of the place was near stifling.

She'd been right where he was. Until her sisters' love brought her back to life.

Determined to get Hayes there too, she moved to the curtains and whisked them open, letting the sunlight spill inside. She turned back, finding Hayes lying curled on his side, looking thin, his hair long, his beard far past scruffy. "You're getting up," she told him. "We're going outside."

When he didn't move, she dropped to her knees next to him. He rolled onto his back and she placed her hand on his chest. "Laurel would be devastated if she saw you like this. You're going to get up and face each day, with me here, until we both have some kind of life worth living."

Tears welled in his eyes. His fingers wrapped around her wrist tight. "I've got nothing left."

"That's not true," she said, hearing the raw emotion in her voice. "You've got me." She grabbed the blanket and yanked it off, paying no attention to the fact that he was naked. She tossed him the jeans that rested in a heap on the floor next to him. "Get dressed. I'm making you breakfast."

Maisie blinked away the memory of the day Hayes had become her friend, instead of just Laurel's husband. They'd come through dark times together, and they had history together. So much history. Some good. Some bad. Some unimaginably painful. But this new thing that had sprung out of nowhere over the last few months made her cheeks hot, and she averted his gaze. What was once friendly between them had become taut with tension that seemed to get tighter every day. This man staring at her wasn't broken anymore. Hunger lived in his eyes. "You need to stay here," she told him. "Let them look you over."

"I'm fine," he said, his voice lower than before.

Not wanting to, but knowing she had to, she slowly took her hand off his chest, watching her fingers drag against the hard muscles, feeling like touching him wasn't all that friendly anymore. "I've been here all day," she pointed out. "You can endure getting looked over."

He held her stare. "Fine, I'll get looked over. But there"—he glared at the nurse—"is no way in hell I'm staying the night."

The nurse turned away, but even Maisie saw her roll her eyes as she left the room.

Beckett laughed.

Maisie nudged Hayes's shoulder. "Be nice. You're really annoying her."

Hayes snorted, lying his head back against the pillow, staring up at the ceiling, that muscle in his jaw twitching again. "Believe me, the feeling is mutual."

🖋️

Hayes counted the tiles on the ceiling to calm the erection he sported from Maisie's touch. Maisie smelled like sunshine and wildflowers, and he hadn't realized how much he liked that smell until one day a couple of months ago. The day that changed everything. His eyes shut as that pleasing scent wrapped around him, bringing him back to the day he realized Maisie was breathtakingly beautiful.

"Right there," Maisie said, standing in Hayes's living room, watching as he moved the couch against the wall across from the big window. "Yup, that's perfect." She smiled and approached. "Dare I say, you actually have a gorgeous living room?"

He laughed. "Yes, I think you can." For the last six months, she'd been helping him shop for furniture. He'd put it off for over a year, but slowly, she helped make his house a home. When he'd moved from Denver, he sold his house with everything in it, except for one box holding all his memories with Laurel. He couldn't go back in the house, not after Laurel's murder.

Maisie plopped down on his new dark gray couch, and the movement caused her cleavage to bounce. His cock, he thought long dead, twitched. "Come on," she said. "We must celebrate with a movie."

His mind went to thoughts of celebrating on his couch...but doing something else entirely. He shoved the thought from his mind and grabbed beers from the fridge before he returned to her, finding her settled back against the pillows. He was certain she wasn't thinking sexy thoughts, but she looked like a French model laid out, ready for him to paint. And he wanted to paint her.

He cleared his throat. "What are we going to watch?" He handed her the beer and then took a seat next to her.

She snuggled a little closer to him, obviously an innocent move, but it didn't feel innocent anymore. He looked around the house. A house that Maisie had helped him put together. She'd been there for him during the darkest times in his life. Until he could actually breathe again, fully. Until he could walk outside and not want to hide. And as she moved closer, he caught her scent, a mix of sunshine and wildflowers. He stared down at her smooth, bare legs, and Hayes knew one thing for certain.

Maisie was no longer just his friend. He wanted more, and he didn't know how to reconcile that with his love for Laurel.

"Today is weird."

Hayes blinked out of his memory, frustrated his erection had only hardened. He turned toward Amelia's voice. His gaze then fell to Beckett, who couldn't take his eyes off Maisie's sister. Beckett and Amelia dated during Amelia's senior year of high school, and Hayes knew for certain the reason Beckett didn't date seriously was because he still loved Amelia. But Amelia had a fiancé now, Luka. Her high school romance with Beckett long behind her. "I agree," Hayes said, glad for the interruption, if only for his hard-on to finally soften. "Today is weird."

Amelia strode farther into the room. "What happened?" she asked, sidling up the bed.

"He fell off a horse and hurt himself," Maisie said before he could answer.

Hayes sighed in exasperation. To Amelia, he explained, "No, I didn't hurt myself. I don't have a single bruise, cut, or anything, but Nash's insurance company requires that when we take a fall, we get looked over by a doctor to get cleared for work again. I'm fine. This is protocol, nothing more."

Maisie's eyes squinted, lit with an inner twinkle of mischief. "He keeps saying that he's fine."

"Which means he's not fine at all." Amelia laughed.

"Ladies," Hayes cut in with a frown, "when I'm say I'm fine, I'm actually fine."

Both of them burst out laughing. Either at him, or with him, Hayes wasn't sure.

Coming to his rescue, Beckett's cell rang.

"It's Nash," Beckett said to Hayes, then lifted the phone to his ear. "Hey, Nash. What's up?" His voice faded as he strode out into the hallway.

Amelia turned to Maisie. "All right, Maisie-Moo, you've been discharged. Ready to go home?" Amelia was the only one to call Maisie that nickname, and as much as Maisie said she hated it, Hayes knew she liked it. Even loved it.

"Thank you, all that is holy," Maisie replied eagerly. Though her attention soon snapped to Hayes. "Unless you want me to stay with you."

He lost himself in the concern in her eyes. Christ, that felt good. A little *too* good. "Nah, you've been here all day. Go home."

Her mouth twitched. "Because you're fine, right?"

"Smart ass." He snorted. "And yes, I'm *fine.*"

She regarded him for a good long moment. Nurse Maisie giving him a quick assessment. She must have finally believed him since she nodded. "Okay. Call if you need anything."

He inclined his head in response, having no intention to call. What he wanted was to get the hell out of there. The smell of astringent, hand sanitizer, and cleaning supplies were giving him a headache that had nothing to do with the fall. The doctor was being cautious. Hayes knew his body. He hadn't hit his head when he'd fallen from the gelding that bucked him off. Nothing hurt. He'd barely even hit the ground before he bounced back up. "Next time we see each other," he said with a smile he hoped was reassuring, "let's avoid ending up in the hospital?"

Maisie laughed. "Sounds like a plan. Hope you get out of here soon." She gave him a little wave, showing off her finger that had been splinted, and left the room, followed by Amelia.

Hayes dropped his head back against the soft pillow. Today sucked, and when Beckett returned to the room with a deep frown, Hayes knew it wasn't about to get any better. "What is it?" he grumbled.

Pity shone in Beckett's eyes. "Nash said to consider yourself on vacation. Ten days."

"Fuck that," Hayes snapped, pushing up off the bed, his cowboy boots hitting the floor. "Did you tell Nash the doctor is just being cautious?"

Beckett nodded. "He wouldn't listen. It's a new policy, I guess. Symptoms of a concussion can show up seven to ten days later. His insurance now requires this for any fall."

"I didn't even hit my fucking head," Hayes snapped. He couldn't sit around for ten days. Silence wasn't good for him. He needed to wake early, exhaust himself, and fall asleep instantly at night. Silence made his memory clearer. Too clear, bringing back all the things that haunted him.

When Hayes reached the door, Beckett said, "You realize you need to be discharged."

Before heading out the door, Hayes grabbed his Stetson cowboy hat off the chair and shoved it back on his head. "I'm leaving. Either you're driving me to talk to Nash or I'm taking a Lyft, but this is happening."

Obviously agreeing for the sake of it, Beckett gestured out to the hallway. "Lead the way."

The second Hayes entered the hallway, the nurse sitting behind the nurse's station called, "Where are you going? You haven't been discharged!"

Hayes didn't look back and marched his way out of the damn hospital. Sure, he'd hear about this later. River Rock was a small community, and he knew that nurse from somewhere but couldn't place her. The gossip train would get ahold of this and run with it, but he didn't do hospitals.

Within minutes, Hayes's ass was planted back in Beckett's truck, and they'd left the hospital behind.

Beckett remained silent until twenty minutes later when they rolled up to River Rock's downtown. Quaint brick storefronts hugged the street. The little town had everything from Blackshaw Meats, which was a division of the Blackshaw family's cattle company; to the local watering hole, Kinky Spurs, that catered to the twenty- and thirty-somethings of River Rock; to the animal hospital and the police station all on the one road. Beckett only broke the silence when they'd passed the police station where Hayes had started his career before moving to Denver.

"She's sweet with you," Beckett said.

Hayes glanced sidelong. "Who?"

"Maisie." Beckett looked away from the road to give Hayes a wide smile. "She's got a soft spot for you."

"We've been friends for a long time."

"Yeah, friends, right."

Sarcasm dripped off Beckett's statement. Hayes snorted. "Got something to say?" He'd been friends with Beckett far longer than he had Maisie, and Beckett didn't miss much.

Beckett shifted against his seat and gave a soft laugh. "Nah, nothing to add here."

Not needing Beckett pointing out that something between him and Maisie had changed, Hayes turned his attention back to the window as thick evergreen trees rushed by. Hayes wanted Maisie. In his life. In his bed. But that would only complicate everything. Besides, Maisie was his dead wife's best friend. There had to be some rule book that suggested that was a bad idea. But he also knew Laurel and was well-versed in her heart. She'd want him to be happy, and in the deepest parts of his heart that would always belong to Laurel, he knew that if he made any other woman happy, Laurel would want that woman to be Maisie.

Hayes shook the thought from his head. The idea was terrible, the complications great. He cared about Maisie. Deeply. She'd pulled him out of the darkest time of his life, and he owed her everything. But she didn't deserve to be pulled into his still-messy life. Especially since there was a lie hanging between them.

One that would destroy everything.

Maisie believed Laurel had been murdered in a robbery gone wrong. That's what the media was told and what the newspapers printed. The truth was, Laurel had been murdered by a gang member on a case Hayes was working.

The lie was so embedded now, even Hayes had trouble finding the truth anymore. He couldn't risk Maisie knowing he kept the truth from her, in fear she'd never forgive him. He couldn't risk losing her.

When Beckett finally pulled into the long driveway that worked its way up to the log house and the barn, Hayes refocused his thoughts. He needed to figure out how to get Nash on his side. Hayes got out of the truck before Beckett could even turn the engine off. He made it halfway to the barn when a firm, "Hayes," was said behind him.

Great. That hard tone didn't bode well for Hayes's plan.

He turned, finding Nash behind him, arms crossed over his chest. "Hey."

While a few years younger than Hayes, Nash could hold his own against anyone. Fit and strong, Nash was a retired bull rider. He had messy brown hair and sharp blue eyes. Next to him, dripping saliva onto Nash's worn cowboy boots, was his loyal yellow Labrador Retriever, Gus.

"Care to explain why you're here," Nash demanded.

Beckett strode by, patting Hayes on the shoulder. "I delivered your message," he said to Nash. "And he didn't listen, like I said was going to happen."

Nash's eyes narrowed on Hayes. "Time off is nonnegotiable. You're taking the ten days. Go home."

Most men cowered if Hayes glared at them. Nash glared back. Hayes had two choices: accept the vacation time or quit. The latter wasn't an option. The job was a good second best to his love of the law. "What will it take for me to lessen that time?" he asked, softening his expression, hoping that worked in his favor.

"A note from the doctor saying one hundred percent that you do not have a concussion," Nash said. "Otherwise, don't step foot on the farm. Clear?"

"Yeah, clear," Hayes muttered. *Fuck.* No doctor would sign such a note. The liability was too much of a risk.

"He's a nasty one," Nash said, obviously changing the subject for Hayes's benefit. Nash studied the gelding out in the field before addressing Hayes again. "We'll start some groundwork with him while you're away, but I take it you want us to leave him for you?"

Hayes gave a firm nod. "You're damn right I do. That horse and I have unfinished business."

Before Nash could reply, tires crunching against gravel

had Hayes glancing over his shoulder. A police cruiser slowly made its way up the driveway.

"Expecting a visit from the cops?" Hayes asked Nash.

"Not that I know of," Nash replied.

When the cruiser came to a stop next to Hayes, Darryl Wilson, the scruffy-bearded, dark brown-haired cop rolled down his window. Not only had Darryl graduated high school with Beckett and Hayes, Hayes and Darryl had gone through police academy together. They'd been close friends until Laurel's death. Hayes couldn't face the reminder of the job he loved and the life he'd never have again. Darryl was also married to Maisie's cousin, Penelope. With his elbow resting on his open window, Darryl said to Hayes, "You left the hospital without a doctor's discharge." Darryl glanced at Nash. "Hey, Nash."

Nash nodded in greeting.

Narrowing his eyes, Hayes folded his arms. "Do tell: How did you find out I was even in the hospital?"

Darryl offered a bemused smile, warming his amber eyes. "Your nurse is the wife of the sergeant."

Damn. That's how he knew her. "Fuck. Whose wife?"

"Matheson's."

Hayes snorted. "And he sent you to fetch me?"

Darryl gave an easy nod. "He figured you'd be less...pissy with me."

They were probably right.

Darryl paused to turn his two-way radio down and then said directly to Hayes, "Listen, this is what I've been told. You can either go back to the hospital and wait for the doctor to discharge you. Or your insurance won't cover the charges and you'll have to pay out of pocket." A slow smile began to spread across Darryl's face. "Matheson told me to let you know that his wife, who is already pissed at you, will be even more pissed if you don't go back because she'll have to do more paperwork. And this will not bode well for Matheson. He told me if you make his life difficult, he'll make your life hell."

Hayes frowned. Matheson was a tough bastard.

A gleam filled Darryl's eyes. "Besides, what's so bad about one night at the hospital? I've seen a few of the nurses there. They'll take good care of you tonight."

Beckett called from field, "He was too busy looking elsewhere to notice any nurses there."

Hayes parted his mouth and then shut his lips tight. He *had* been looking elsewhere. He'd only seen Maisie in that room.

Darryl's brows rose. "Oh, yeah, who's got you wrapped up?"

"He's talking out of his ass." Hayes nearly snarled at Beckett, who only grinned back. To Nash, Hayes added, "Keep me updated on the gelding."

"Of course," Nash replied.

Hayes gritted his teeth but got in the damn cruiser. "Don't look so damn happy about this," he said to Darryl, fastening his seat belt.

"But I am happy," Darryl said with a chuckle, turning the cruiser around. "I just won a hundred-dollar bet."

"On?" Hayes inquired.

Darryl grinned. "If I'd require backup or you'd come willingly."

Hayes dropped his head back against the headrest and shut his eyes. "I should have punched you."

"The day's not over yet." Darryl laughed and hit the gas.

3

The next morning, Maisie woke before her sisters and made it outside unnoticed. After Pops passed away, and when the plans for the brewery began, they'd all moved back into their grandfather's house. Financially it made sense, at least until the brewery took off, and she doubted any of them would be leaving anytime soon. And truth was, being in that house had been Maisie's saving grace after Laurel passed away.

Once on the road in her MINI, she drove the twenty minutes to downtown and parked at the curb, hurrying out to greet the sunny morning.

Downtown River Rock was as close to postcard-perfect as Maisie had ever seen, with the vast mountain range encasing the town. She didn't bother locking her car but took her purse with her and hurried inside Snowy Mountain Bakery, where she was immediately hit with the overwhelming aroma of sugar and warmed bread.

Susan, an adorable elderly lady with purplish curls atop her head, smiled from behind the counter. "Maisie, my dear. How is the finger?"

Maisie resisted rolling her eyes. News traveled fast in River Rock. She lifted her hand, showing off her splint. "All bandaged up. I'll be good in no time." But even with the painkillers that Clara brought home last night, her finger *hurt*. And this morning, while she watched the sun rise over the mountain peaks through her window, she began to wonder how she could pull the festivals off with a broken finger. There was a booth to set up, kegs to move, beer to serve.

Susan's brow wrinkled. "Oh, I'm so glad to hear you're okay. I'm not sure what you were even thinking moving around those big kegs all by yourself."

Great. Not only did everyone know about the accident, but now they knew how clumsy Maisie was. Perfect. "Well, I use a dolly. I'm not exactly lifting them. The keg just got away from me this time."

"It's so heavy," Susan continued in a clipped voice, like she hadn't even heard Maisie. "That's a man's work."

Now wait just a...

"Mom," Annie, Susan's daughter, snapped at her mother when she came out from the back. "I'm sure Maisie is completely capable of doing her job well." Annie's soft brown eyes held Maisie's and she mouthed *sorry*.

Maisie shook her head. No harm, no foul. Susan was a sweet woman and meant well, but she was born in a different time, raised with a different mindset. One that Maisie thought needed a refresher course, but Susan wasn't her family.

Annie stepped up to the counter and gave a gentle smile. "What can we get for you, Maisie?"

"A dozen assorted muffins, please." Maisie needed to pull out the big guns this morning. Yesterday was a disaster.

She needed a fresh start, and baked goods always put her sisters in a good mood. Even Clara.

A few minutes later, muffins in hand, Maisie was back on the road and headed home. When she finally arrived, the driveway was empty. Later today, cars would line the small parking lot next to the barn. Three Chicks Brewery was part of the brewery tour put on by local companies for vacationers. Maisie had loved doing that job, but her cousin Penelope took it over. Because, well, Penelope was better at being on time, being responsible, and not letting kegs fall on her hand. Heaviness sank into Maisie's chest. She didn't mean to suck so much at her jobs, she just got easily distracted. Sometimes it seemed like the world was out to get her, like a keg breaking her finger.

She parked next to Clara's practical sedan and Amelia's bright blue Yaris. The scent of the fresh baked muffins surrounded Maisie as she hurried into the house, greeted by the nutty aroma of fresh brewed coffee coming from the kitchen. She found her sisters sitting around the old, worn oak kitchen table looking at their phones. "I have sugary awesomeness," she said by way of greeting.

Both sisters were off their butts in a second flat.

Mason, Clara's son, came running in from the family room. "Me first. Me first."

"Well, of course, fine sir." Maisie opened the box, and he took the apple cinnamon muffin before bolting away.

As Clara reached for the muffin, she said, "I think it's safe to say he probably doesn't need the sugar."

"Sugar is always good," Maisie said with a smile.

"I agree," said Amelia, taking the box of muffins over to the kitchen table near the bay window.

Maisie quickly made herself a coffee with cream and then joined them. She took the first bite of her peach streusel muffin and sighed in happiness. "Oh, my God, this should be illegal with what it's going to do to my ass."

"Ditto." Amelia chuckled.

"Ha! I knew there were muffins." Penelope entered the kitchen, wearing her long brown hair up in a messy bun. Her olive-colored blouse did amazing things for her green eyes, but Maisie thought it was probably happiness that made her look so alive. Penelope and her husband, Darryl, were madly in love, and Maisie had never been happier for her. Penelope had crappy parents, who shipped her off to River Rock for the summers. A blessing, really, since there, with Maisie's grandfather, Penelope saw what real love was like. Maisie and Penelope had always been kindred spirits. Her cousin grabbed a muffin from the box and took a seat next to Clara. "I swear I could smell them from the driveway," Penelope continued. To Maisie, she asked, "How's the finger?"

Maisie rolled her eyes. "It's just a broken finger. It's not like I cut an arm off or something."

Penelope's brows rose. "Touchy subject, I take it?"

"Mortifying subject," Maisie mumbled, taking another bite of her muffin.

Clara blessedly—or maybe not so blessedly—cut in, "All right, let's chat about tomorrow's festival. I need to stay home with Mason. Amelia's brewing tonight. Penelope's got a tour to run." Maisie felt everyone's gaze zero in on her, as Clara added, "Since none of us can go with you, have you figured out how you're going to handle all this? You've got to bring a lot of gear to the events, along with the kegs."

"Of course, I've thought about it," Maisie lied breezily. The festival itself she could handle. The setting up was the problem. But—and this was the biggest *but* of all—she didn't want to admit any of that to her sisters. They were nailing this brewery stuff. Even Penelope who had no stake in the brewery, except to work there, had the beer tours running like clockwork. No mishaps. No accidents. Maisie simply needed to catch up. And fast. "You don't need to worry about anything. I've got it all figured out."

Clara gave a glassy stare. "Really? What's your plan, then?"

Maisie cleared her throat. She hadn't gotten that far yet. She'd only thought as far as muffins to put her sisters in a good mood. "Well, I...ahh..."

"Why don't you ask Hayes to help you?" Penelope interjected.

"Hayes?" Maisie repeated.

Penelope nodded. "Darryl told me last night that Nash told Hayes to take ten days off to make sure he's not suffering a head injury."

Maisie tilted her head to the side, her thoughts freezing for a second. "Wait. Darryl talked to Hayes?"

"Yeah," Penelope said, unwrapping her muffin. "He drove Hayes back to the hospital last night."

Maisie shot up from the table, her mouth dry. "Is Hayes okay? What happened?"

"Okay, hold up there, Batman," Penelope said with a smirk. "He's fine. He just jumped ship and left before he was discharged. I guess the nurse helping him is the wife of one of the big guns at the station. You know what they say, happy wife, happy life...well, his wife wasn't happy. If Hayes hadn't gone back, it was going to mean lots of paperwork. I guess it was their anniversary, and it would have made her late for their dinner."

"Oh, shit," Maisie said, returning to her seat.

"Aunt Maisie said shit," Mason called from the living room.

Across the table, Clara glared. "Really?"

"Sorry." Maisie cringed. She was never a good influence on Mason. "That's a bad word," she called to him. "Never say that word ever again."

He ran into the kitchen. "But you just did." His cute, six-year-old eyes were twinkling.

Clara pointed a finger at her son. "Never say that word again, Mason. Do you understand me?"

He screamed words Maisie didn't even understand as he ran back into the living room.

Maisie avoided Clara's gaze and asked Penelope, "Did Hayes actually go back to the hospital?"

Penelope shoved a piece of muffin into her mouth. "Yup, he stayed the night and was discharged this morning."

Amelia said, "Bet Hayes was thrilled about that."

Penelope nodded, her mouth twitching. "Darryl said he was in quite the mood when he left him last night."

Hayes was always in a mood, and not usually a good one. Well, to others. Hayes was grumpy most times, but not with Maisie. She liked that, knowing she made things better for him.

"Mason, no!" Clara lurched up as Mason dove in for another muffin. He belly laughed when she grabbed him around the waist. "Okay, it's school time for you. Say bye to your aunts and Penelope."

"Bye." Mason wiggled out of her arms and then made a fart sound before running out of the room.

Clara sighed after her son then looked back at the group, rolling her eyes. "Fart noises and laughing about poo is my life now."

Amelia and Penelope laughed.

Maisie said, dead serious, "It could be worse. At least it's not about killing things, ghosts, or his desire to cut anything open."

Clara scrunched her nose and slowly shook her head. "Seriously, Maisie, I don't know how you do it, but I can always count on you to make me feel better in weird ways."

"Of course you can." Maisie smiled. Mason, while a total handful, was a really good, sweet kid. And Clara was the reason for it. She was an amazing mom. Uptight and a little stressed at times, but a damn good mom, especially considering she was raising Mason on her own. Maisie had long suspected that the father was Clara's high school sweetheart, Sullivan Kenne. Even Amelia was convinced the now-professional baseball player was Mason's dad. But Clara wouldn't ever admit to it. After a while, the conversation never came up again.

"Mason Carter get back here right now," Clara called in her *mom* voice. "We need to talk about the fart noises."

When Clara's voice disappeared after she left the house, Penelope added to Maisie, "Honestly, I think you'd be doing Hayes a favor by asking him to go to the festivals with you. He doesn't really seem like the type to just sit around and do nothing. Maybe a road trip is right up his alley."

"Maybe," Maisie agreed. But the moment the thought entered her mind, her belly filled with butterflies. Three nights *alone* with Hayes...

As if reading her thoughts, Penelope grinned. "Unless there is a reason you don't want to be alone with him?"

"Of course, there is isn't," Maisie said, heat rising to her cheeks.

Amelia gave a sly smile. "Mm-hmm, sure. We all believe that."

"Oh, hush, both of you," Maisie said, taking a muffin and putting it in a Ziploc bag, realizing that apparently she had been showing her feelings a little too much lately. Feelings she hadn't even totally figured out yet, considering that mixed in with her attraction for Hayes was also a bucket load of guilt for feeling anything for Laurel's husband. "Hayes and I are friends," she said to everyone, including herself.

"Right, just *friends*," Amelia said. "Who's that muffin for?"

Maisie refused to look at them as she pressed the bag closed. "If I'm going to ask Hayes for a favor, I need to bring him a treat, don't I?"

She nearly made it out of the kitchen when Penelope burst out laughing and called, "Hate to break it to you, Maisie, but I don't think that's the muffin Hayes wants."

❧

When the Lyft dropped Hayes off at home at a little after ten o'clock in the morning, his throbbing headache from being awakened every hour to ensure he didn't have a concussion worsened. Waiting in the circular driveway was his father, leaning against the SUV with POLICE CHIEF written on the driver's side door. The gossip train had obviously filled his dad in on the fall yesterday, but Hayes didn't even want to know how his father knew he was on his way home from the hospital. Hayes shared his father's strong build, only his dad was slightly shorter, with darker brown eyes and a salt-and-pepper beard that matched the hair on his head. There was nothing soft about his father, including his stare as he looked upon Hayes.

"Thanks for the ride," Hayes said to the driver before slamming the door shut.

"Most people call their family when they've been hurt,"

his father rebuked, arms crossed. He wore his typical small-town uniform of business casual pants, tan cowboy hat and a navy-blue polo shirt.

"I wasn't hurt," Hayes reported, sidling up to him. "I had a fall. It wasn't a big deal, but Nash requires the hospital visit for insurance reasons. A call wasn't warranted, believe me."

His dad scanned Hayes from head to toe. "Not hurt, then?"

"Not even a little."

His father's frown only deepened. "I don't know why you're bothering with these wild horses. If you're out to kill yourself, I can think of better ways to do it than putting yourself through repeated hospital visits."

Hayes did them both a favor and didn't deny it. He took risks he knew he wouldn't have before Laurel died. In the last sixteen months of working for Nash, he'd gone to the hospital for stitches above his eyebrow, a relocation of his shoulder, and to get fluid drained from his knee, and that was only recently. The first eight months after Laurel died, he couldn't even leave his house until Maisie showed up. "Like I said, the fall wasn't bad."

"What's this, the second hospital visit in six months?" his father countered.

"Third, actually," Hayes corrected.

His father's expression softened, his strong hand cupping Hayes's shoulder. "I'm not exactly sure what you're doing with these horses other than punishing yourself, but don't you think it's time to stop it?"

Hayes glanced out to his red brick bungalow, with black accents and a matching roof. The flower bed hugging the walkway had been Maisie's touch, as was the flowerpot resting by the front door—with the gold lion door knocker —that she repotted every spring. When Hayes returned home to River Rock, he'd bought the property with half of Laurel's life insurance policy. The rest of the money was sitting in an untouched bank account. The only reason he bought the property was for the mature weeping willow tree that rested on the edge of the creek. Weeping willows were Laurel's favorite, and Hayes had spread her ashes there, exactly where she would have wanted, giving her the perfect resting place that, in life, she would have loved. "This is my life now," Hayes finally said, glancing back to his father. "You're going to have to accept that."

Dad frowned, slowly removing his hand. "Laurel wouldn't want this. Getting yourself hurt all the time isn't going to bring her back."

"I know that," Hayes shot back, heat building in his chest.

"Then come back to the force," Dad countered gently. "You don't need to work in Denver. Come work for me, in town. You're a damn good cop, Hayes. That's where you belong."

The radio in the SUV crackled, and the dispatcher's voice rambled off a radio code. That high-pitched voice was like an anchor, yanking Hayes back to the night when Laurel's life ended, reminding him why, no matter how much he missed being a cop, he couldn't ever go back.

"10-32 at 420 Mill Street," the dispatcher called along the radio waves.

Hayes and the other cops were celebrating the arrests of five punks who unleashed a reign of terror on Denver. Men and women had been beaten and robbed. A few cars set on fire. The last of their crimes involved a banker, who had been abducted for the money he had access to at the bank. Now those bastards were behind bars, and the residents of Denver could sleep soundly again. Well, mostly. They still had cops out searching for the leader of the gang, Earl Falik, who'd gotten away with a gunshot to his shoulder from Hayes's weapon.

Hayes had a split second to decide if he'd kill Falik or disarm him. Hayes went with the latter, and the second after the bullet sliced through Falik's shoulder, Falik said through gritted teeth, his ice-blue eyes dead and cold. "You'll pay for that."

Falik smiled a deadly promise, and it looked like the devil was grinning at Hayes, when Hayes was suddenly hit from the side. He hit the pavement...hard, his head smashing against the concrete. Darkness crept into his vision as Hayes fought against Falik's cousin, watching as Falik ran away.

Hayes never should have let Falik run. He should have shot him dead.

In the station, when Hayes heard the address come across the radio, he finally understood what Falik meant, and Hayes's fucking world blew apart. The code the dispatcher used meant man with a gun. And that address was Hayes and Laurel's home.

Not knowing if his fellow cops were following him, Hayes sprinted to his cruiser and pressed his phone to his ear while he gunned it down the road, the blue and red flashing lights cutting through the darkness. "Answer, Laurel. Dammit, answer." Four times, he'd tried calling. Four times, she didn't pick up. "Fuck." He threw his phone to the car's floor. He'd thought he'd felt fear, pain, and worry before in his life, but not until this moment did he truly understand those emotions. And they left him reeling.

When he reached his house, he drove up onto the grass of his lawn. His neighbors screamed at him from their houses as he ran from the cruiser. They were obviously hearing the gunshots, but too afraid to come any closer. Hayes couldn't make out what they said past the thundering of his heartbeat. Gun drawn, he noted the front door was locked, so he moved swiftly around the back of the house. There, he spotted the back door open. He slowed his breathing, shoving hot emotions down deep into his gut as he entered the house.

Each step he took felt like a lifetime until he reached the bedroom. Time stopped, then. Everything stopped. His life ended when he spotted the blood dripping off delicate fingers and onto the hardwood floor.

Hayes's stomach roiled, and he sucked in a harsh breath, yanking himself back from the memory he'd tried to forget. The night after he found Laurel dead in their bedroom, Hayes had hunted Falik, and after a shoot-out, Falik was dead. Hayes left law enforcement after that. He couldn't go back to it. Face that old life. Face his pain. "I left the force for a reason," he reminded his father. "Please don't make me explain this again."

His father studied Hayes and then sighed. "I know, but you can't keep running from this and working yourself into the ground because of it. You need to forgive yourself for what happened. Laurel would want that."

Hayes couldn't forgive himself. Laurel was gone. Had he taken the shot he should have, Laurel would not have been targeted. She would still be alive. The thought left a sour taste in Hayes's mouth, and his stomach knotted as he caught the sound of tires crunching against gravel. He glanced over his shoulder, finding a black MINI with a red roof coming up his driveway. An unexpected release of tension rushed over him. He shoved his hands into his pockets, hiding their shaking.

Maisie parked next to the SUV and got out of her car. "Hi, Mr. Taylor," she said, a ray of sunshine. "How are things?"

"Doing good, Maisie." Dad returned the smile and gave her a quick hug. Everyone loved Maisie; she was impossibly happy. Always. Her smile was infectious, and even Hayes felt an unexpected grin pull at his lips.

"Glad to hear it," she replied to his father. Then she glanced at Hayes and she bit her lip, studying him intently. "Everything okay?"

Hayes nodded. *Better now that you're here.*

Obviously, done with the fatherly lesson he'd come to give, Dad tipped the rim of his cowboy hat at Maisie. "I better be on my way." To Hayes, he added, "You'll think about what I said?"

Hayes inclined his head as his answer, instead of flat-out refusing. His life as a cop was in his past. No going back.

Once his father's SUV was halfway down the driveway, Maisie whistled. "Wow. The tension between you two was near stifling. What's up?"

Hayes gestured for Maisie to follow him over to the Adirondack chairs on the small stone patio near the flower garden. "He wants me to come work for him."

She sat next to him, her eyebrows raising over her sparkling baby blues. "I had no idea you were considering being a cop again."

"I'm not," he clarified, stretching out his legs, resting a boot on the big rocks around the firepit. "My father thinks I'm wasting myself at the horse farm or determined to kill myself."

"You won't hear me disagreeing with him there."

Hayes's brows shot up. "You think he's right?"

She gave a little shrug. "Only someone looking to punish themselves would take the risks you do."

Most times he liked that Maisie always cut through the bullshit. Whatever came to her mind came out of her mouth. For him, being so tightlipped, he found her openness refreshing. Only he didn't much like it directed at him. "I'm not punishing myself."

She gave him a knowing look. "What would you call it, then?"

"Doing the job no one else wants to do," he managed.

She snorted a laugh. "Yeah, because it's really dangerous, and seeing that you're doing it without wearing full body gear like Beckett told you to, I'd say you're doing it to hurt yourself."

"You think I'd hurt myself on purpose?"

"Yes."

He recoiled. "Seriously?"

She gave a firm nod. "Sometimes when we hurt inside and can't deal with that, we make our outsides hurt instead." She glanced away and changed the subject. "Do you think you'll ever go back to the force?"

He still reeled from her earlier statement and barely managed, "No."

"That was a quick answer."

He shrugged. "I don't need to think about it. Being a cop was another life."

"Did you tell your father that?"

Hayes nodded. "He just happens to disagree with me."

She watched him a long moment. "Well, I knew you as a cop, and I know you now, and you know what?"

"Do I even want to know?"

Her smile filled the hollowest parts of his chest. "I liked you as a cop. And I like you as a horse trainer, even if I seriously question your sanity. So, I say you just keep doing you. Your dad will simply have to deal."

Hayes felt the tension slowly melt away. "Want to tell him that?"

"Ha," she said with a grin. "Don't dare me. You totally know I would."

Yeah, she would. Nothing stopped her, even when faced with a situation where she knew she might not come out on top. "I'm afraid of what you'd do if you unleashed on him. My father hasn't met honest Maisie."

"He probably wouldn't like her," she agreed with a laugh. "You know, you being the son of police chief and all, I'd probably get in a whole lot of trouble."

He winked. "Don't worry, I'd bail you out."

"Good," she said. "I'm glad to know you wouldn't let me rot in jail."

"Never. You've got me. Anytime you need me."

She smiled.

Hayes looked at his boots on the rocks lining the firepit. Even if Maisie knew he missed being a cop, she couldn't know *why* he would never go back. He couldn't stand the heartbreak that would fill her eyes when she found out Laurel hadn't died because they'd been robbed. He couldn't hurt Maisie like that, not after she finally seemed happy again. She smiled all the time like she used to. She laughed just as much. But most of all, Hayes needed her. "How's that finger?" he asked, changing the subject.

She blinked and looked down at her finger, stuck between the metal brace and tape. "It's a reminder that I really suck at this whole brewery thing."

"Accidents happen," he offered. "Nothin' you can do about that."

She lifted her stare to him again and gave a cute smile. "Funny you should mention that, because there is actually something I can do about it. And that something involves you."

"Me? How?"

"Yup, *you*," she said with a nod. "Penelope sort of mentioned that you had some time off. So, I've got a mega favor to ask, and please don't say no." She pressed her palms together as if she were praying, holding them tightly to her chest. "Clara already tried to fire me, but she's agreed to give me one more shot. I've got three beer festivals to do over the next four days, starting tomorrow."

"All right," he said. "But how does this involve me?"

She grinned. "Because I need muscles. Big, strong muscles."

He couldn't fight his smile and arched an eyebrow at her. "Are you inflating my ego to get me to agree to go to these festivals with you?"

"Is it working?"

He chuckled, shaking his head at her. Yeah, it kind of was. "What exactly would you need me to do?"

"Oh, good," she said, bouncing in her seat. "Okay, so you'd help set up the booth and take it down at the end of the night." She waved her broken finger at him. "Let's be honest here, I struggled setting up before. I'm clumsy on a good day. And now with a broken finger, there's just no way I can pull this off by myself." She gave him puppy-dog eyes. "So...what do you say?"

He took in those sweet eyes. That desperation on her face. The way both of those things ruined him. "Does anyone ever say no to you?"

She gave a firm nod. "Yes, Clara does all the time."

He wasn't sure how. Hayes couldn't find the strength to refuse her anything. He sighed. "When do we leave?"

She squealed, jumped up from her chair, and threw her arms around him, bringing her soft curves against him like they belonged there. Heat blasted through him, making him fully aware of every spectacular inch of her body. Her coconut-scented shampoo infused the air, and he restrained his groan at the soft press of her breasts against his chest, of how damn good she felt there.

When she backed away, he noted there was heat in her eyes too. "Come to the brewery tomorrow morning at nine o'clock, we'll leave from there," she said.

"All right." He forced his attention onto her face, instead of letting his gaze sweep over her as he so desperately wanted. "See you tomorrow, then."

"Bye." She turned, and he could have sworn she put an extra wiggle to her hips.

The groan he'd been fighting slipped free, and he immediately stood, heading for the house to deal with what she did to him.

4

"*Sweet home Alabama, where the skies are so blue,*" Maisie sang to the music blasting through the speakers the next morning. She sat next to Hayes in his big-ass *loud* truck, while he drove down the sunbaked road, looking like some hunk out of a country music video. She'd offered to drive the brewery's truck but got a flat *no*. He hooked his truck up to the trailer with the THREE CHICKS BREWERY logo written on the side and off they went to their first stop, Fort Collins. He'd rolled down the windows almost immediately, forgoing the air conditioning on the blistering hot day, so she stuck her feet out the window, the sun warming her toes. "*Sweet home Alabama. Lord, I'm coming home*—hey!" She shot Hayes a glare when he turned the volume down. "I love that song. Turn it back up."

Hayes put his cowboy hat on the dash. "Sorry to tell you this, but we're nearly at the festival." He glanced sidelong at her, arching a brow before turning his attention back onto the road. "It might be useful to stop singing and talk about what's ahead of us tonight."

She shuddered, invisible creepy crawlers rushing across

her skin. "Ew, you sound like Clara. Take that back right now."

His loud laugh filled the cab of the truck. "The fault of *that* lies on your shoulders. You've brought me into this. Now I can't fail, or I'll have to face your sister's wrath."

Maisie laughed, wiggling her toes against the hot breeze brushing over them. True. She loved Clara, but her older sister could destroy anyone's personal armor with a single look. "Okay, you're right," Maisie hedged, pulling her feet back into the truck and sitting cross-legged on the seat. "We probably should talk about what's ahead of us." She reached into her tote bag with all her art supplies.

"Whatever happened to that?"

She glanced up, finding Hayes gesturing at her tote.

"Back in the day, I remember you wanting to open up an art studio."

Her heart squeezed. "You remember that?"

"Why wouldn't I?" he asked, eyes on the road. "You and Laurel talked about it for a year straight in our living room."

The reminder of her past life with Laurel didn't hurt like it used to. Now warmth touched those cold, grief-stricken places, and she noticed over the last few months, Hayes could talk easily about Laurel too, recalling all the love, the joy Laurel had brought to their lives. For as long as Maisie could remember, she and Laurel had talked about opening the studio together. Well, a coffee shop/art studio that, even though it didn't sound like it would fit in town, they'd planned to make work.

"Plans changed," she told him, knowing he'd understand.

And he did. "Yeah, they do." He scrubbed a hand over his face.

An ache filled her chest, and she wished that were something they didn't have in common. "I haven't even thought about the art studio in so long. It's kinda one of those dreams that wasn't ever meant to be," she explained. "The brewery is my life now."

Out the window, wind feathered through the wild grass and crops as he gave her a quick look. "A bit of a shame. You're so talented."

"Thanks." She smiled. "But it's a hobby now, nothing more. My sisters have a lot on their plates, and I haven't been helping their stress." She opened her notebook. "I've got to keep doing my part to make the brewery a success."

"You're on your way to the festival, aren't you? I'd say you're doing your part."

She chuckled, flipping through a bunch of papers trying to find the one where she'd made notes about the festival. "Let's have that conversation at the end of the festivals after we've nailed this."

"What exactly are you looking for in there?"

She flipped over a few more pages of doodles. "I made notes about what we need to do, just have to find them."

His soft laugh drew her gaze. "That is how you keep notes?"

She glanced down at the ripped-out pages, covered in paint. "Hey! One woman's mess is another woman's treasure."

He gestured to her notebook. "Those notes are your treasure?"

"Damn right they are," she said, lifting her chin. "Ah, here it is. Okay, we've got three festivals. First one, as you already know, is in Fort Collins, then we hit Colorado Springs, and Boulder to finish up."

He nodded, taking that in. "Tell me why these three festivals are important for the brewery?"

"They're the three biggest festivals in Colorado. It's a great way to market beer and showcase our brand, or so Clara told me. She's already entered Foxy Diva into a bunch of contests, but mainly, these festivals are all about word on the street, which Clara said is really important. I guess it's good to get buzz going on social media, so when we finally reach out to a distributor, we've got a solid proposal."

"So Clara says?"

"Bingo." Maisie laughed.

The rich floral aroma of hardy wildflowers carried through the hot breeze as Maisie flipped the page, looking at the back. "Ah, yeah, okay, so basically we need to get there and set up our booth. I'll serve beer all night, if you don't mind switching out empty kegs for new ones."

"That is why I'm here." He smiled. "The muscles, remember?"

Dear God, how could she forget? Her belly somersaulted at the heated smile he threw her way. Which was both confusing and delicious all at once. There would always be a part of her heart that hated this new growing attraction she felt for Hayes. Some part of her that would always feel like she was being a horrible friend to Laurel. But as she stared at Hayes now, he looked different than he did when Laurel was still with them. Or maybe Maisie didn't used to notice him in that way. But now, thirty-one years old, with the wind rustling his hair, his arm resting on the window, his thumb guiding the steering wheel, wearing worn jeans and a black T-shirt, Hayes looked *hot.* Yummy hot. The truth was, Laurel was never coming back, and while Maisie fought her growing feelings for Hayes for a while, ignoring those feelings was becoming harder. Especially when she saw Hayes responding to the heat too.

The more time went on, the more Hayes went from

being Laurel's husband, to Maisie's friend, to...well, she'd only gotten so far as accepting that her desire for him was a very real, palpable thing that could no longer be controlled. But she hadn't figured out what to do about it yet.

She glanced back out the front window and finally answered him, "It really shouldn't be too difficult, but—"

"Nothing is ever easy when you're involved?" Hayes offered, his mouth twitching.

"Exactly." Which was, of course, mortifying. She really meant to make it to places on time, to do the job the right way, but it never seemed to work out. Something *always* went wrong. This time, it simply could not. One last chance. That was all she got to make Pops proud.

Though, as she studied Hayes next to her, she smiled. He seemed to understand and accept her just like Laurel and Penelope always had. He didn't see her flaws as faults, but saw them as quirks. She liked that.

The rumble of a truck ahead drew her gaze up, and Hayes slowed his truck as they passed a construction crew. She covered her nose at the pungent scent of hot pavement and tar in the air. When they cleared the construction, Hayes said, "Those are good, you know."

"What are?"

He gestured at her doodles. "Your art. That's your thing. Don't forget that."

"You haven't seen my work in years. How would you know?"

A mischievous glint hit his eyes. "I saw your painting in your car when I came to the brewery the other day."

"Oh." She shifted a little in her seat, twisting the white gold wildflower ring on her right ring finger. "So, ah, you liked it?"

He glanced sidelong. "I thought it was beautiful."

Heat radiated through her chest, spiraling down to places that seemed to be heating a lot more when Hayes was around. She turned her head, hiding her smile, and took it all in. The plane flying overhead, the bright sun and blue sky, even the wooden fences around the cow pastures off in the distance. Maybe this was going to work out after all...

A loud bang had her grasping her seat belt, making sure she wasn't going anywhere, when Hayes slammed on the brakes. "What's wrong?" she gasped.

"I suspect we've got a flat." He groaned, pulling over to the side of the road.

Oh no. Things couldn't be going south already.

Hayes's warm hand slid onto her thigh. "Maisie."

Her breath caught, and it wasn't over the stress that they might be late. The heat of his touched burned right down to her core, making her want that touch to move higher up her thigh.

His soft stare held hers. "It's just a flat tire, not a bad omen that everything's going to go wrong."

"Right." She plastered on a fake smile and lied through her teeth, pretending she didn't want to rip his clothes off. "Right. Not a bad omen."

❧

Hayes rolled the truck into Fort Collins only an hour later than planned. He stopped by a garage and picked up a new tire, instead of driving on the spare. They drove through the old historic neighborhood with houses from the 1800s, and even passed by a vintage trolley, until they reached the university, where buildings turned large and modern.

In the university's parking lot, Hayes stopped next to the rows of trucks and trailers belonging to the best craft breweries in Colorado. He noted Maisie's bouncing knee, realizing this had to be scary as shit for her. Brave little thing she was, and he'd always liked how she faced challenges head-on, even knowing that it was very likely she'd fail. He was determined as hell to make sure this time, no matter what, nothing went wrong. "Ready to do this?" he asked her.

She took a calming breath and then smiled brightly at him. "Yup, let's go make this festival our bitch."

Three hours later, as far as Hayes was concerned, Maisie had done just that.

People strode around the stadium carrying cups of beer. The noise level was near deafening. Between the loud hum of the crowd, and the rock band in the far corner putting on a show, Hayes could barely hear himself think. The mix of spilled beer, sweaty bodies, and grease lingered in the air.

In their corner of the stadium, the Three Chicks Brewery logo was printed on everything: the banner, the backdrop hanging off the booth, the sleek wooden jockey box cover that kept the beer cold, and Maisie's tight black tank top that hid nothing and revealed *everything*. Hayes now wore a matching T-shirt, only his was roomy. The Foxy Diva logo was on the bottle openers, buttons, and other swag that the crowd snatched up quickly. While Hayes was impressed by the set-up, Maisie herself blew him away. She had owned this event, doing what she always did—making every person feel special simply by talking to them. Every customer laughed or at least smiled by the time they turned away with their Foxy Diva in hand. Clara had made the right call by putting Maisie in charge of festivals. She was...*captivating*.

So much so that she'd gained the attention of four men sitting at a picnic table kitty-corner to the Three Chicks Brewery's booth. They'd already been up to the booth once to get beers from Maisie. Hayes ground his teeth at the attention coming her way. That tall, lanky guy wasn't interested in the beer, and Hayes had seen enough creeps working as a cop that his internal alarms were going off. There was only one thing worse than an arrogant prick. A drunk arrogant prick.

His teeth began to hurt when he finished attaching the hoses on the jockey box to the new keg. Until tonight, he hadn't even heard of a jockey box, but he'd learned from Maisie that it was a mobile draft beer system built into a standard insulated cooler. Once the keg was attached, the beer traveled through coils that cooled the beer leading to a draft faucet for pouring.

When he rose, Maisie said to a customer, "Save water and drink beer, I always say."

The older gentlemen raised his glass and gave her a wide smile. "Fine words, my dear."

As the man turned away with his wife, Hayes sidled in next to Maisie. "You're better at this than you think you are."

"Yeah?" Maisie asked, her face upturned. "I feel like all I'm doing is just serving beer. I don't know... Should I be doing more?"

Hayes shook his head. "You're being yourself, and you've got the people eating out of your hands."

"God, I hope so," she said in obvious relief. Applause erupted near the band as she grabbed a rag to wipe up the spilled beer on the jockey box cover that had a Foxy Diva bar tap faucet. Once done, she tossed the cloth back into the bucket of sudsy water, wiped her hands on her jeans, and then grabbed her phone from her back pocket.

Hayes attempted not to notice the tightness of her tank top. How a thin line of skin showed when she lifted her phone. He failed miserably. Christ, she was sexy as hell.

"Okay, looks like you might be right. I'm actually not doing terrible," she said, drawing his attention back to her face. "We've got a couple hundred or so more followers on Instagram and Facebook. Looks like that tag-us giveaway seems to be working."

"The tag-us giveaway?"

"It's an idea that Amelia came up with. If you looked at the swag"—she nudged her shoulder into him—"then you would have seen the sign that she had made. Anyone who takes a photograph with a glass of Foxy Diva and tags us on social media, is entered to win ten cases of Foxy Diva at the end of the three festivals."

"Good idea," he said.

"Yup, brilliant." She didn't seem bothered that the idea hadn't been hers, and was glad to give credit where it was due. She took a couple of steps backward until she stood in front of the backdrop. She took hold of his T-shirt and tugged. "Come on. A picture at every stop to remember the time you totally saved my ass."

He chuckled, settling in next to her. Her wildflower scent enveloped him, filling every bit of air he had, as he wrapped an arm around her back and leaned down to get to her height. Her warm body pressed into his. She felt strong and somehow soft too. Like she stood on own her two feet and could kick some ass, but that when she needed and wanted, she could give in and let go. He'd never known how much he liked that combination until right now. She angled her head toward his, her beautiful smile filled his vision as she snapped the picture.

When she moved away, Hayes was glad for it. Heat flooded his groin, need hitting him with such intensity he fought against the instinct to pull her into his arms again and... *Pull it together, man.*

He thrust a hand through his hair, but sudden coldness stole any heat Maisie brought. The creeper who'd been watching Maisie before approached her. The hunger in the guy's eyes grated on Hayes's last nerve.

"Hey, sugar," the guy said.

Hayes restrained his snort since he bet Maisie found the guy attractive. He looked athletic. Confident enough, likely making him good with the ladies. And his hair looked like a modern cut, obviously a city guy, with a beaming white smile to finish off his good looks.

"Back again already," Maisie said with her sweet smile. "Good beer always brings 'em back."

The guy nearly purred, "Especially when such a pretty lady is serving up the beer."

Now Hayes held back the roll of his eyes. Maisie was far too smart to fall for this guy's bucket of bullshit.

"It helps when her customers have charming smiles," she said.

Hayes jerked his head toward her, finding her leaning against the bar, squishing her breasts together, maybe not on purpose. But Hayes noticed. And so did the guy.

The creep gave her a smile that didn't look charming. He looked like a damn snake. They exchanged flirty small talk while Maisie poured the beer from the tap, and the guy's eyes lingered too long on her breasts.

"Enjoy your beer," she finally said, handing him the plastic cup.

"Believe me"—he winked—"I'll be back for more."

She smiled.

Hayes snorted loudly.

Once the guy walked away, Maisie slowly turned toward him, eyebrows raised. "Problem?"

"He's not right for you."

"Oh, really." She crossed her arms, smirking. "Are you telling me you know the right type of man for me?"

"Yeah." He gestured at the prick walking back to his douchebag friends in the sea of people. "It's not that guy."

The announcer called over the loudspeaker, and the crowd erupted in whistles and catcalls, as Maisie said, "Trust me, right now, any guy is the right guy. If you haven't noticed, there hasn't been anyone new to town in a while." She studied the guy at the table, who watched her right back. "I mean, he's cute, in a fancy way."

Every instinct in Hayes screamed *creep.* Having no real way to explain that, Hayes went a different route. "Yeah, if you want a guy who spends more time looking in the mirror than you do."

She burst out laughing, placing her warm hand on his arm. "Now I really can't be with someone who is prettier than me."

"Exactly." Hayes smiled, fully aware of her touch. Of how he wanted that touch to move lower. "Take that guy." He flicked his chin at the man in camo ordering a beer from the booth across from them. "He's good."

Maisie followed his stare and then frowned. "Hayes Taylor, what is wrong with you?" she snapped, glaring at him. "I'm twenty-four years old. I want a heartthrob that will break my bed, not a guy who looks like my old science teacher."

Hayes shrugged. "Looks like a good guy." Or maybe he just didn't look like an attractive guy.

She turned to him fully and gave him a hard look. "Remind me to never, and I mean *never,* ask you to help set me up with anyone."

Fine by him. He laughed softly, but then gestured back

at that guy. "Do me a favor tonight. Just stay away from that one."

"You've got a bad-guy radar?"

He nodded. "One that's seldomly wrong."

She watched him a long moment, and he had a minute to wonder when in the hell he'd become so protective over her. Jealous too. Fuck, that was a problem. A big one. This went beyond physical. He could control his body, refuse to act on his impulses. But this warm spot she had grabbed hold of in his chest, *that* was much harder to ignore.

Her soft smile told him she didn't mind his concern. "Fine. Deal. As long as you promise to *never* set me up."

The promise was easy. "Deal."

❧

When the kegs dried up and the crowd began to thin, empty beer cups littered the picnic tables and cement floor, and the stench of vomit hung in the air. Maisie breathed through her mouth, trying to avoid the pungent aroma, and unhooked the keg from the jockey box. The heaviness of her eyelids suggested it was far past midnight, the set time the festival had meant to close, and she was ready to call it a night, glad Hayes was there to help her pack up. The motel wasn't too far. No doubt Clara had booked a place nice enough to keep Maisie safe, but cheap enough to keep Clara's frugal ways satisfied. At the moment, a bed, no matter how hard or bumpy, sounded good.

Maisie's broken finger throbbed as she set the empty keg aside when her phone beeped. She needed painkillers. Pronto. She looked at the screen, unsurprised to find Clara checking in. How did it go?

Maisie texted back with her uninjured fingers. You

tell me. Clara would have been stalking social media all night, making sure Maisie didn't screw things up. Even Maisie was still waiting for the bomb to drop. It always dropped.

Big thumbs up on social media. Amelia's giveaway idea rocked. Buzz looks good.

Maisie sighed, a weight on her chest that she hadn't realized had been there lifting. Great. Event seemed to go well. People were happy.

I see that all over social media. But you know what I'm seeing more than that?

Maisie winced. "Hopefully something good," she muttered to herself.

Clara's text popped up. People posing with you for photographs. You make everyone feel like they're your friend. Be proud of that, Maisie. Good job tonight.

Warmth carried through her, and she fought the tears welling in her eyes. Not being a disappointment felt...*good*. For two years now, she'd struggled. Every single day she tried to do the right thing for the brewery, but somehow seemed to fail. This time belonged to her, and maybe...just maybe...this was all finally going to work out. With the help of Hayes, of course. She texted back: I am proud. Thanks. I couldn't have done any of this without Hayes. He's been awesome too.

Clara responded, Thank him for me too. Keep it up. You're rocking this! Love you.

Love you too. Sweet dreams.

With this new sudden lightness in her chest, Maisie drew in a long, easy breath, tucking her phone back in her pocket.

"You look happy."

She glanced back at Hayes, taking in the strength of him, the solidness of his character. God, those eyes damn near melted her panties off. He stepped closer, bringing all that power into her space. "I take it you've heard good news."

She nodded, clearing her throat, placing herself firmly back into the friend zone. "Clara's happy with everything that's being shared on social media."

His smile was totally Hayes. Undoubtedly supportive and sexy as hell. "That is good news."

"It is," she agreed. "Only two more to go, then I can actually breathe again."

Hayes took another step closer, the air infusing with his scent, a mix between the Colorado countryside and the first taste of spring. Her breath hitched, cheeks warmed, and his mouth twitched up at the corners in response. There, so close, he dipped his chin, bringing his gaze down to hers. "You were very good tonight. These festivals are right in your wheelhouse."

This close to him, she became fully aware of the little space between them. That if she took a step and lifted her chin, her lips would meet his. "That might be true, if you didn't do all the heavy lifting."

He gave her his easy smile. "There's nothing wrong with needing help. I don't think even Clara would have objections about that."

Probably not, but Maisie didn't want help. Clara and Amelia didn't need any. Maisie had something to prove, and by the end of this, she hoped she would prove it. Not only to her sisters, but to Pops too. She shrugged, not letting her ego get the best of her. "I guess you're right."

Her doubts clearly played out on her face as his reply was immediate. "It's going to be all right, Maisie. We'll see this through. Get this done."

The stableness of Hayes was so damn sexy. So was the trust between them, and even their solid friendship. She never had that with any other man before. Hayes *knew* her, fully, all the good, all the bad, all the broken and the healed. Her belly fluttered, heat pooling low in her body. Her gaze shifted to his lips, and she licked hers, wondering how he tasted. How he kissed. Was he soft and gentle? Or did he take charge? Maybe both? And why was she even thinking about this?

She quickly looked away, moving out of his space and to the front of the booth to pack up the remaining swag.

Behind her, Hayes cleared his throat. "What else do you need me to do here?"

She refused to lift her gaze. He'd see the lust there. She'd see his lust, and then what would happen? "This last keg and the jockey box can go out to the trailer. It shouldn't take long after that to take apart all this, and then we can hit the road. The motel is a good twenty minutes from here..." Then a thought—a slightly terrifying one—hit her.

At her silence, Hayes asked, "Problem?"

Confident that the lust was now snuffed out, she faced him. "I'm so sorry, I just realized I never called to get another room booked for you. There's probably not one available with the festival in town."

Something devilishly naughty crossed Hayes's expression. "One room is fine. I know how to keep my hands to myself."

The desire she thought she'd controlled slammed into her, forcing her to squeeze her thighs together at the steady pulsating there. Hayes's attention went straight to her thighs, and when he lifted his gaze again, those eyes of his were dark. Her mouth begged to open and say, *What if I don't want you to keep your hands to yourself?* Instead, she laughed awkwardly. "Right. Okay, well, let's get all this packed up and get on our way. I'm exhausted."

"Sounds like a good plan." Hayes's forearms flexed in ways that should have been illegal as he grabbed the empty keg and jockey box. He had a lot going for him. Albeit, it'd been a long time since she'd seen him with his shirt off, but his forearms had grown bigger and harder since he'd worked at the horse farm. She was not immune to the effect those muscles caused. "Be back in a few," he finished.

She nodded, holding it together by taking a deep breath. The joke was cruel—she finally found a man who made her *want* and want *bad*, and made her *feel* and feel *hard,* and by appearances, he felt the same way, but he had yet to make a move. And she was too confused by it all to make the move herself. Would they complicate things? Was it wrong they felt this way?

Her heart told her no. Laurel would want them to be happy, especially if that happiness was found in each other. But Maisie's head was all kinds of messy. Because if it was okay for them to be together, and if Hayes was feeling the heat between them too, why hadn't he made a move?

Tonight, he seemed...jealous. It didn't take much to realize he didn't want her dating anyone. But then if he was jealous, why wasn't he speaking up? Hayes wasn't a quiet guy. Or a shy guy. A man who didn't take what he wanted. The more she thought on it, the more she realized, maybe she simply wanted him so much she made herself believe he wanted her. It wouldn't be the first time she'd gotten something so wrong.

Determined not to let herself get distracted from what mattered now—the beer festivals—she began untying the backdrop and taking it down. Focused on her task, she was startled when a low voice sounded *very* close behind her. "Hey."

She whirled around, finding the guy with the charming smile. He stood close enough that she could smell beer and cigarettes on his breath. "Hey." A slight chill shivered over her as she looked for Hayes. He was still gone, and when she looked back into the dark, glazed brown eyes in front of her, she got the feeling this guy had waited for exactly that. She slid away from him and settled in front of her booth.

The guy followed her. His voice was low, seductive. "You should ditch that guy and we can go somewhere."

"Thanks, but no. It's been a long day." She scanned the area again, finding most of the booths had packed up and left, only a few stranglers on the other side, like her, who worked at their own speeds.

The guy stepped even closer now. Too close. "Ah, come on, sexy," he purred. "You'd have a fun time, I promise."

She noticed his crew of guys were moving in their direction, and suddenly, what seemed like flirting became something different. Coldness crawled up her spine like an icy spider. "Listen, it was nice to meet you, and thanks for the interest in the beer, but in case you can't take the hint, I'm not interested."

She went to move away, but he latched onto her arm, his fingers pinching. "Ah, don't be like that, beautiful."

She winced against the brutal hold. "Ow. Let—"

His hand was ripped away and the guy suddenly went soaring, landing on his ass. Hard.

She jerked her gaze to Hayes, his feet planted wide, his stance at the ready. His snarl was nothing she'd ever heard from him before. "Does that help you understand she's not fucking interested?"

Maisie blinked. Blood poured from the guy's nose.

"Fuck," he growled, cupping his face. "You broke my fucking nose."

Another blink, and the guy's friends were rushing over. Maisie took in Hayes's corded neck, the lifting of shoulders as if readying for a fight. "Do not even think about it," she said, pointing at him. "There is only one of you and four of them."

Hayes's gaze flared. "I'd say I'm sorry I'm not going to listen to you, but we both know I'm not."

Then he charged into the group of angry, drunk men.

5

"That was stupid," Maisie said, dabbing the small cut under Hayes's right eye. He sat on the end of one of the double beds in the Durango Lodge, the budget-friendly motel with mountain views. Silence was a hard find. The water gurgled within the pipes and half-heard conversations spilled in from people passing by the door. But the place was clean, and the television worked.

Another dab of the cloth had Hayes fighting a flinch. That small cut was the only evidence of the fight that hadn't lasted long. Nor was it a fair fight, and Hayes knew that when he charged forward. Being a trained cop, in both self-defense and some martial arts, he allowed himself one punch to the bastard who'd put his hands on Maisie. The others in the group he'd taken down easily since they all were drunk. Security had swarmed in quickly, kicking everyone out, including him and Maisie. His only regret: he hoped Clara didn't get wind of it. But protecting Maisie, defending her, he didn't regret that.

Maisie removed the cloth and said firmly to him, "For

future reference, I really don't need you guarding me and going all Captain America on assholes."

He chuckled. "Captain America?"

Using the soft washcloth, she dabbed again and gave him that cute smile back. "You flattened their asses like some Marvel character. Seriously, where did you learn how to fight like that?"

She thought he kicked ass. Fine by him. But... "One, none of them knew how to fight. Two, they were all drunk. Three, they're cowards. It was hardly a fight." He pointed to his cheek. "That was a sucker punch."

She made a noise in the back of her throat and continued to dab the wound.

Hayes liked this. Her attention. It had been so long since a woman had taken care of him. He'd forgotten how nice the sweet touch of a woman felt. To not have to exist alone. To have someone else to depend on. Yeah, he liked that.

"I've got no doubt you can handle yourself," he explained, "but that doesn't mean that when some dickhead puts his hands on you and you flinch in pain, I won't fix it."

Her smile stopped Hayes's world from turning. The softness of it, the affection, all the things he couldn't even name. For months now, he'd been fighting his desire for her. Right here, right now, he wondered what she'd do if he didn't.

Would she run?

Would she kiss him back?

"Well, thank you for looking out of for me," she eventually said, pulling the cloth away. His hand gripped her wrist before his brain caught up to him. The moment his fingers tightened around her warm skin, her cheeks flushed deep, and she visibly swallowed before continuing, "Thank you for being here. For helping me with the festivals."

And there, in the depths of her eyes, he found his

answer. She'd kiss him back; he was sure of it. "You don't have to thank me, Maisie. I want to be here." He slowly dragged his fingers along her wrist, assessing, but not before feeling the hammering of her pulse beneath his fingers.

Heat flooded his groin. "Besides," he said, hearing the need in his own voice, "it felt good to unleash some tension on someone who actually deserved it."

Her hooded eyes lifted to his. "You, tense? Never."

He scanned over her pouty lips before lifting his eyes to hers. "Hilarious."

She gave him that cute smile before setting the washcloth on the dresser and grabbing the ointment from the first aid kit she kept in the trailer. She dabbed the ointment onto the wound. He wanted to do the right thing, to say the right thing every step of the way with her, but his gaze fell to her parted lips and he hungered to feel that pouty mouth against his. For a few seconds, there weren't muffled voices through the door, there was only them and the sweet way Maisie tilted his head up. "There." She examined the wound then smiled at him. "All better."

He wasn't sure if it was the heat pulsating between them, or the realization he made tonight, but he didn't want to stop where things were going with them. He didn't want her looking for another guy. He wanted her looking at him. Only *him*. He reached for her hand and felt her go still as he threaded his fingers with hers, pulled in by something he could no longer control. "You take such good care of me, Maisie." He glanced up into her eyes, finding them soft and warm. "I've never thanked you for that. Told you how much I appreciate everything you've done for me."

Her chest rose and fell with her heavy breaths. "You don't need to thank me."

"No?" He stroked his thumb over the back of her hand,

heat flooding him at the way her lips fell open, begging for his kiss. "You never expect anything back, do you? No matter how much of yourself you give."

Her parted lips shut and opened again with her shudder as he kept stroking his thumb across her skin. Under her fierce stare, he allowed the desire he felt for her to flood him, to finally show her right where his head was at. "I didn't like seeing that guy put his hands on you. I wanted to hurt him."

Her gaze held his intimately. "I'd say you achieved that."

He looked down at their held hands, watched his thumb slide back and forth over her creamy skin. "I don't think I'd like to see any man put his hands on you."

"Okay..." she said softly, obviously trying to understand where he was going with this.

He closed his fingers in hers and looked up. "We never asked for this, you and me. Never expected any of this."

"No, we didn't," she agreed softly.

Wanting her to feel something good in a world that had made them both feel pain, he cupped her face. She leaned into his touch, her hair falling on the side of her face, her teeth nibbling on her bottom lip. "I'm tired of not acting on the way you look me."

"How do I look at you?" she rasped.

"Like you want me to kiss you."

Her breath hitched, the only response he needed.

He wasn't wondering if this was a mistake, he was only thinking that he couldn't run from this anymore. Tonight, he'd seen enough. He didn't want another man anywhere near her. That was the one truth in front of him. He couldn't look away anymore. "I'm tired of fighting this, and I suspect you are too."

She didn't ask what he meant; she simply licked her lips, readying them for him.

He stroked her soft skin. "Fighting what's been brewing here for months." He caught the heated surprise in her eyes, but every guard was down. They weren't just friends, but something more. Something that was hungry and urgent, that demanded to be fed. He fought back a moan, his cock hardening to steel as he slid a hand across her hip, pulling her in between his legs, needing her closer. "Only question is whether it's time to act on it or not."

He expected a response. But the one she gave surprised him. She cupped his face and brought her lips to his.

Maisie knew with the soft press of her mouth against Hayes's that they were stepping into dangerous new territory, but there was no way in hell she planned to stop. And when Hayes threaded his fingers into her hair and gave a low growl from his throat, there was no turning back. She'd wanted this. Wanted him. She climbed onto his lap, his hard length resting between her thighs, promising her the pleasure she'd craved for months. His lips traveled to her neck, his heavy breathing brushing across her ear. She unabashedly ground herself against him, needing *more,* wanting all of him. A moan spilled from her when his free hand came to her hip, his strong fingers guiding her faster, harder against him, like they were teenagers, scared to take it to that next base, but fiercely determined to get each other off.

But she wasn't a nervous teenager. And neither was he.

Hayes grabbed her tank top and pulled it over her head. With a flick of his fingers, her bra followed, and his callused fingers took her breast. His tongue stroked her nipple before his lips sealed on the taut bud. Her head spun in a thousand directions, asking a million questions, but falling into the pleasure of the moment too...until he lifted his head. His gaze met hers. She was afraid he was going to stop, but she found solidness there, strength. Lost in the swirling whiskey depths of his eyes, she remembered she knew this man. Knew all the good things. Probably knew most of the bad. She never dreamed he'd look at her this way, with hot obsession. His dark eyes yanked her out of her head and into this new space they created together, the hot need pulsating between them. She realized why he hesitated now and what exactly he waited for.

Her permission.

Not wanting to wait a second longer, she grabbed his T-shirt. He had it over his head before she could even lift it up fully. His arms wrapped around her then and he flipped their positions like she weighed nothing at all, hovering over her.

The strands of his hair hung over his forehead as she cupped his face. He stared at her. Hard. With lust practically vibrating off him. "You sure you want this, Maisie?"

She slid her hands down over his neck, his wide shoulders, chest covered in soft dark hair, admiring each and every groove of his six-pack. It'd been two years since she'd seen him at the lake with his shirt off, and Hayes's body had changed, becoming stronger. Thicker, more muscular. A man's body.

"I want you," she told him.

The low moan he gave made goose bumps rise across her arms. "Good, because fuck, I need you."

His unleashed desire only heightened hers. She brought her hands between them and reached for the button on his jeans and quickly lowered the zipper. This time, when his mouth met hers, his kiss was different. All consuming. A man's primal hunger. He bit her lower lip before sucking it into his mouth. His tongue stroked hers. His lips matching her rhythm perfectly, like he'd been kissing her a lifetime. All those questions needing answers slowly began to disappear as she lifted her hips, grinding against him.

"Don't stop that," he told her, watching every swirl of her hips. "Fuck, Maisie. Yeah, don't fucking stop that." He reached into his back pocket to grab his wallet, extracting a condom. In the next breath, his jeans were down, and his thick cock sprung free.

Maisie took him in. Every single gorgeous inch of his straining, hardened length. When she lifted her gaze to him, her breath vanished at the uncontrolled fervor staring back at her. She reached out, desperate to feel him in her hand. His eyes slammed shut, head fell back as she stroked the soft, silky skin over hardness, feeling the warm liquid escape the tip. Using that lubrication, she worked her hand over him slowly, delighted by his eager moans.

When his heated stare finally returned to her, his jaw clenched. He stepped out of her hold to remove her jeans and panties. Once she lay naked there for *him,* he froze.

A beat passed. He gazed between her thighs then slowly looked up...and up... "Maisie," he murmured. Soft, affectionate, warm, and she melted as his hand stroked over her belly. "You're beautiful."

Her heart fluttered. "Not so bad yourself, cowboy."

She thought he might chuckle. He didn't. His brows pulled together as he kept stroking her belly. "I never knew..." His smoldering gaze lifted to hers when his hand slid between her thighs. "Damn, stay just like this. Let me watch you."

Her eyes fluttered as he stroked her sensitive flesh slowly, gently, and she arched back into the pleasure when he dragged a finger through her folds. He grunted when he noticed how wet he'd made her. "Fuck yeah, you're so damn sexy, Maisie." She opened her eyes, finding him hovering over her. He slid one finger inside her, and she dragged her hands up his forearms, feeling the incredible strength of those hard muscles.

She reached for his cock and stroked him. Once. Twice. Before his mouth met hers again with a delicious growl, the kiss deeper this time. Faster. Harder. He devoured her until they were both breathing deep. He broke away only to rip open the condom, sheath himself, and then he grabbed her hips and yanked her bum off the bed. He wasn't polite and gentle. No, he did precisely what she wanted.

He entered her, right to the hilt. He moved slowly at first. Until he hooked her legs over his shoulders. Then he gripped her hips, the bed squeaking beneath her, the headboard slamming against the wall as his thrusts became everything she needed and more. He drove pleasure into her, rounds of hard and fast thrusts stealing her breath away. Her eyes shut against the sensations taking her under, stealing away the view of Hayes's gorgeous face and straining muscles. He began pumping harder. Faster. Until the world drifted away and his roar of pleasure followed hers.

Many, *many* minutes later, she managed to make her mouth move. "So, that happened," she said.

Hayes's low chuckle rushed over her. He now lay next to her, his chest rising and falling with his heavy breaths. "It most certainly did."

Breathless, too, she glanced sideways at him, finding his eyes closed. "Did we just complicate everything?"

He turned his head and opened his eyes. "No, it means we wanted something, and we took it."

She swallowed the emotion that crept up, an unsettling feeling rolling though her stomach that this thing between them couldn't be that easy. Blessedly, before she had time to think about it more, her cell phone beeped. She reached for it on the nightstand where she'd left it and looked at the screen. "Shit."

Hayes leaned up on one muscular arm. "What's up?"

Maisie was tempted to lick that bulging bicep and the vein running along the side. Reminding herself that she was in trouble, she threw on Hayes's T-shirt and sat cross-legged on the bed next to him. "Oh, you'll see," she finally managed to say. Then she accepted the FaceTime call and smiled into the phone. "Hello, Clara."

Clara's ponytail was a mess, makeup smeared under her eyes. "Are you two out of you goddamn minds! A fight?" she snapped. "Seriously? What the hell happened?"

Maisie sighed. "Well, I..."

The phone was suddenly ripped away. Hayes arched an eyebrow at Clara. "Someone made unwanted advances on your sister tonight and grabbed her arm hard enough that she flinched. I didn't like that. The blame for this is on me, not on Maisie."

A pause. "I see. Can you put Maisie on the phone please?"

Maisie fought her smile at Clara's very serious voice. She accepted the phone. "Yes?"

Clara's eyes were huge. "Is Hayes in your bed right now?"

Hayes lay back down, all man, all muscles, stretched out in the bed and grinned. "Mm-hmm," she said, looking back at Clara.

Clara fought her smile. "Let's talk more tomorrow—"
Hard bangs suddenly came at the door. "What's that?"

"I dunno," Maisie replied.

Hayes jumped out of bed, slid into his jeans, and
grabbed a T-shirt from his bag. When he whisked the door
open, Maisie's heart dropped into her stomach.

"Um, Clara, we need to go."

"Why?"

Maisie took in the two men in uniform, the guns on
their waists, and the dark irritation in their gazes. "The
police are here." She ended the call, even though she could
hear Clara calling out to her.

The taller cop said, "Hayes Taylor?"

"Yeah," Hayes said, opening the door wider. "What's the
problem?"

The cop stepped into the room, taking Hayes's arms
behind his back, and then cuffed him. "You're under arrest
for the assault..."

Voices became a loud roar in Maisie's head. Regardless
that she only wore a T-shirt that just covered her bare butt,
she jumped out of bed. "Wait. He didn't do anything wrong.
That other guy was the aggressive one."

The other cop pointed at her and scowled. "Sit back
down or you'll be coming with us too."

"It's all right," said Hayes, his expression soft, reassuring.
His voice calm. "Call my father. His number is in my phone.
Passcode is 1209."

Laurel's birthday. December 9. Maisie stepped forward.
"But—"

Hayes sent her a smile that chased away the chill. "Keep
that bed warm for me. I'll be back soon."

Unsure what to do, she followed him out the door as
they took Hayes to the cruiser. Unsurprised by this develop-

ment—because shit always went wrong—she shut the door and hurried to Hayes's cell that was now on the floor; obviously it had bounced off the bed. When she found his father's contact, she hit call.

"You better be dead or hurt to call me this late," Hayes's father said by way of greeting.

"Um, sorry, Mr. Taylor, it's actually Maisie."

A pause. "Maisie. What's wrong?"

"There was a situation earlier. A fight. Blood. A broken nose. The cops just showed up." She hesitated, reining in her babbling. "They've arrested Hayes and took him to the station."

His father asked in a clearer voice, "Where are you?"

"Fort Collins."

"I'm on my way."

The phone line went dead, leaving Maisie growing colder by the second, knowing that once again, everything she touched turned to disaster.

6

The stench of old coffee and sweat mixed with the sounds of telephones ringing and doors buzzing overwhelmed Hayes's senses. Closing his eyes, he rested his head against the hard metal bars of the jail cell. A drunk man slept on the floor across from him, having thrown up three times in the steel toilet. A teenage kid cried in the far corner. Last night, the cops hadn't asked questions, they'd simply hauled Hayes into the station and left him sitting there ever since. Hours had passed, and Hayes felt every one of them. Politics had to be at play if it took his father this long to get him out, and Hayes wondered who exactly he'd punched last night. But that wasn't his biggest concern.

Maisie.

He'd clammed up when Maisie had asked if they'd complicated things. Of course they had. Because he couldn't be the man she needed. The one who'd protect her. He was the guy who'd lied to her. Who never told her the real reason Laurel was dead. The last thing he wanted to do was hurt her, and he wasn't sure he could do anything but that.

And yet...*and yet*, he needed her, like the air he needed to breathe.

"Interesting night?"

Hayes smiled and opened his eyes. His father stood on the other side of the bars, with a uniformed cop next to him. "You could say that." He rose, approaching the cell's door. The cop nodded at the camera over his shoulder. The jail cell beeped and then the door clanged open. "What time is it?" Hayes asked as he strode out into the hallway, leaving both the kid and the drunk behind.

Dad looked at his watch. "Just after two o'clock."

Damn, they'd held him long. The aches in his back and neck told Hayes he'd been there for hours, but he hadn't thought it'd been for nearly fourteen hours. He kept the thought to himself while he gathered his belongings from lock up and followed his father out the front door. Only when the bright sun warmed his face did he address his father. "Let me guess, the dipshit I punched wasn't just anyone."

Dad's keys jingled as he unlocked his SUV. "He's a lieutenant's son." Before moving to the driver's side, Dad stopped, folding his arms. "Want to tell me what happened?"

"The guy got handsy with Maisie last night."

Dad's brows rose. "And that warranted a broken nose?"

"Ah, good, I broke it." Hayes hadn't been sure, even with the blood. He grinned at the slow shake of his father's head. He wouldn't apologize for the punch—the prick deserved it and Hayes hoped his nose killed this morning—but to clarify, he added, "His hold was tight enough that she flinched." Done with explaining himself, Hayes shifted the conversation. "How was Maisie when you saw her this morning?"

Her pained gaze when the cops took Hayes away had stayed with him all night.

His father's gaze turned probing, his eyes searching. Whatever he found must have erased the remainder of his concerns. "She was worried but settled when she heard me laying into the lieutenant after she'd told me her side of the story."

"And what was her side of the story?"

Dad gave a beaming smile. "She's thinks you're a goddamn hero."

"Not a bad way for her to see me." Hayes chuckled. "Though I imagine she was just trying to get me out of jail."

"I don't know about that, son," Dad said. "There was a ring of truth to it."

Hayes glanced down to his worn boots and kicked a pebble away. To avoid talking about this new development with Maisie, he asked, "How many strings did you have to pull to make this go away? Do I owe anyone a favor?"

Dad opened the door to his SUV. "Not many strings, and no favor owed." He got in, and Hayes slid into the passenger seat as his father continued. "Maisie told me this morning that you've got two more festivals to go to." He turned on the ignition and gave Hayes a leveled look. "Let's not punch someone at every one, all right?"

Hayes snorted. "Believe me when I tell you the prick deserved it."

His father didn't comment on that but opened the glove compartment. He offered Hayes his phone. "Maisie left this for you."

Hayes looked at his screen, not finding any calls or texts. "Where is she now?"

"She fought with me for a good hour about leaving you, but after a call from Clara, she drove your truck to Colorado

Springs and is setting up for tonight's festival." Dad pulled out into the road and then smiled over at Hayes. "I'm under strict orders to take you there. She's a force, isn't she?"

Hayes laughed and nodded. "She may be little, but she is fierce."

"That is very much true with all of the Carter sisters," Dad noted.

Hayes agreed and glanced out at the wide-open country, taking in the harvested round hay bales. His thoughts went to Maisie. Her naked body filled his mind. The soft curve of her breasts, her smooth, flat tummy that led down to soft curly hair. God, she was beautiful.

"All right?"

Hayes jerked his head toward his father, the images of Maisie in the throes of pleasure gone as fast as they'd come. "Yeah, I'm good. Last night was an annoyance, nothing more." No matter how much his father pushed him to return to the force, at the heart of it, his father did so because he thought it was right. His father had been a great dad growing up; supportive, attentive, there for him, even more so after his mother had moved away after their divorce. Hayes still had a great relationship with her. She called often. He visited her when he could.

Dad gave a sideways glance, a knowing smile. "I'm not talking about the fight."

Damn. Obviously, Hayes couldn't control the expression on his face. He needed to fix that before he saw Maisie again.

"That's still up for debate," he admitted.

"Anything you want to talk about?"

"Not particularly." But as soon as the words left his mouth, he regretted them. He'd always told his father the truth. "It's..."

"Complicated?" Dad offered.

Hayes snorted. He'd told Maisie last night it was anything but complicated between them. "Yeah, you could say that."

"Because she was Laurel's best friend?"

Warmth touched Dad's tone, and Hayes looked his way, spotting that same warmth in his face. He'd loved Laurel. Everyone loved her. "Part of the reason."

"What's the other part?"

Hayes glanced out the window, staring out at the whiskey barley fields that rushed by. "You know why."

Of course, Dad called him out. "Because she doesn't know the truth about what happened?" A pause. When Hayes didn't reply, Dad spat, "You're an idiot."

Hayes scowled at his father. "Am I?"

"Yes, son, you fucking are." Dad's jaw tightened, eyes on the road, fingers white around the steering wheel. "You were dealt a brutal blow. Now you've got this sweet, bright woman who has been there picking you up, when we all know, life would have gone dark for you otherwise. And now, instead of making yourself and her happy, you're too afraid to tell her what happened so you can finally move on. When did you become such a coward?"

Hayes drew in a deep breath to stop from lashing out. His father didn't deserve it, especially when every single word was the truth. "What good will telling her the truth do? Bring up all her pain again. Too much time has gone by."

"You're telling me this *isn't* about you being afraid because you're terrified she'll hate you for it?"

He cringed at the truth his father hit him with.

Dad slammed on the brakes, skidding the SUV to a halt on the side of the road. He threw the truck in park and then set his firm gaze on Hayes. "You've hated yourself more than anyone could for something that was never your fault. You're not the only one who lost Laurel. I don't blame you, and Maisie wouldn't either. This is your pain. Your shit to get figured out." His father pointed at him. "You might want to start figuring that shit out so you don't go around punching drunk idiots because you're keeping all this bad shit inside you."

Hayes arched an eyebrow. "Done?"

Dad narrowed his eyes. "You've got one shot at life, buddy. Yeah, I see you're wasting it, wallowing in your pain and punishing yourself, but unless you're all in with Maisie"—he leaned in and pointed at Hayes again—"keep your hands off of her."

Hayes knew that, as much as his father thought the world of Laurel, he thought equally as highly of Maisie, maybe even more so, because of what Maisie had done for Hayes when he was at his lowest. And the Taylor men protected the women they cared about. "Yeah, got it."

The Colorado Springs beer festival held a different vibe than Fort Collins. The event was held outside in a large park, with each booth adding a little sparkle to gain attention across the dark night. Maisie had brought Edison string lights, and with the plants she'd picked up on the way, the Three Chicks Brewery booth looked romantic, chic and dreamy even, compared to the very masculine tents around her. She supposed that was her artist's touch, to find beauty where there wasn't any and showcase it.

"You're making everyone else look like they don't know what they're doing."

That low baritone of Hayes's voice brushed over Maisie, causing her breath to hitch. She spun around and all but tackled Hayes, throwing her arms around him. "Oh, my God, you're okay."

His warm chuckle hit her as he bent his head, bring his mouth against her neck. "I'm all right," he told her, holding her close.

Any worry that things might have been awkward when they saw each other instantly fled. They were good, she felt that in the strength of his arms locked around her. She held on, longer than she normally would. "What happened?" she asked, leaning away.

He took her hand before she could move away, his fingers twining with hers. "Nothing much," he explained. "Those cops were just throwing their weight around because that guy I punched was the lieutenant's kid."

She studied his face, not finding any strain there, then released the tension in her own chest with a deep sigh. "I'm so glad you're okay. I felt terrible leaving this morning, but your dad promised me he'd get you out." She averted her gaze to the booth across from her, shifting on her feet, her stomach in knots. "Clara would have killed me if I didn't make set up on time."

Hayes tucked a finger under her chin, demanding her attention. She greeted his gentle eyes, the stare he seemed to give only to her. "You did the right thing by leaving. The festival takes precedence, and honestly, I'm fine. Please let it go."

"Okay, fine, I will," she said with a laugh, finally letting herself off the hook. Responsibility sucked. She wasn't very good at it most days. But she had this one chance to prove she could see something through. That she mattered to the success of the brewery. "You're right. I've got to stay focused."

He gave a firm nod of agreement, then turned back to the picnic table behind him and offered a white takeout container. "We passed a smokehouse driving in. Hungry?"

"Lord, yes," she said, hurrying to sit down. Because of the delay on her leaving this morning, she hadn't had a good meal all day, only a bag of chips, a Coke, and a chocolate bar on the drive.

He sat next to her, opened up his container, revealing brisket, ribs, pulled pork, and an assortment of side dishes. "Did you manage setting up all by yourself?"

"Yeah, right." She laughed and opened the lid. She nearly purred in happiness at the meat, cheese grits, and corn bread before gesturing to her right. "That guy over there helped out. His name is Ralph."

When Hayes followed her gaze, she noticed Ralph, who was around her age, was looking right at her. Well, more like sizing up Hayes.

She glanced back at Hayes to find the corners of his mouth twitching. "Another suitor I need to punch?"

"Please don't." She nudged her shoulder into his, completely aware of those hard, capable arms. The strength they possessed. With warmth pooling low in her belly, she remembered what those powerful muscles could do to her body. She cleared her throat, refocused. "Besides, we've got a busy night ahead of us. The festival opens up in a half hour." Hopefully, all that heat flaring through her would only burn hotter later tonight once they were at the motel. She took another bite of her corn bread and then hopped up and poured them a couple beers, offering him one before she took her seat again. She nibbled a small piece of corn bread and added, "So, tell me, how was jail?"

He ate half of the corn bread in one bite. "Annoying," he said with a full mouth.

She snorted a soft laugh. "Do you get in extra trouble or something because you're a cop?"

"*Was* a cop," he gently reminded her. "And yes, I'd be up shit's creek if I was still on the force, but I'm not, so it's fine."

She watched him for a long moment. "Do you ever miss being a cop? You know, the excitement of it all?"

"Why would I?"

She shrugged. "Because for as long as I've known you, you always wanted to be a cop. Or at least that's what Laurel told me."

He studied her, assessing, before he explained, "You're right. Being a cop was always my dream job. I come from a long line of cops, so it's kind of in my blood. But working for Nash is good too. I needed a change after Laurel passed away. I couldn't go back to that life."

Maisie nodded, remembering how Hayes had been when she'd first walked into his house that day and found him so utterly broken. "I get that. Laurel's death was hard for me too." She hesitated, then quickly corrected, "I mean, not as hard as it must have been for you—"

"You loved her too," Hayes interjected gently, reaching out to comfort her with a hand on her arm. "Laurel was in your life longer than mine."

"Yeah, she was," Maisie drawled, thinking of how things had been for her after Laurel passed away. "You know, that's what was the hardest. If something happened good or bad, I'd always reach for the phone to call her, but then I—"

Hayes flinched.

"Sorry." She reached for his hand on her arm, tangling her fingers with his, squeezing gently. "We can talk about something else."

"Nah, it's all right." He grabbed her hand again when she began pulling away. Eyes on her, he placed a kiss on the back of her hand before letting go. "Talking about Laurel is good. It's nice to remember her and not only see pain."

Maisie reached for her fork. "I think so too. My sisters really pulled me out of the dark time. So did Penelope. They filled that void. Became the friends I needed."

"Which is what makes pulling these festivals off so important to you?"

"Exactly." She scooped some cheese grits onto her fork, liking how easily Hayes seemed to understand her. "I'm not sure where I'd be if it weren't for my sisters and Penelope. And while the brewery was never really my thing, I don't want to fail them, not after they were there for me." At Hayes's understanding nod, she continued. "Clara's the brains of the brewery. Her ideas are just incredible. And Amelia is the reason Foxy Diva is such a hit. It took her months to perfect the beer, altering my grandfather's recipe. Now it's my turn to do my part."

"And you're doing it," he said reassuringly.

She shrugged slightly. "I'll breathe a lot easier when these festivals are over. Clara will have what she needs to push ahead to find a distributor for the beer. And my part in all this will be done." Then she'd have to figure out what to do next within the company. Maybe she could take over the social media and marketing since they were gaining more followers.

"We'll get there," Hayes stated. "See this through."

Her chest expanded, air a little easier to drag in. He watched her in a new way, with a little more curiosity and a lot more heat, and she liked it. She ate the cheese grits, wondering what Laurel would think of all this. Her with Hayes. She guessed from her friendship with Laurel, her friend would say, *"The guy you're with isn't the Hayes I knew.*

The husband I loved died when I did. He's someone different now. Someone you like. Just be happy."

"Can I ask you something?"

She glanced up, finished her bite. "Sure."

Hayes's expression turned probing. "Why have you been single for so long? You dated when Laurel was alive. Had that one boyfriend for a year."

"Seth?"

Hayes nodded. "Yeah, that one. Whatever happened to him?"

She hesitated, wondering if she should share, considering the truth may hurt. Deciding the truth mattered above all else, she explained, "After Laurel passed away, I changed. Hell, everything changed. I began to take things more seriously, and I think it all got too real for him. Too dark, I think."

"So, things got tough and he bailed?"

"I know it seems harsh, but I couldn't really blame him. Things went from super fun to super sad. All I did was cry. He wasn't looking for that. He wanted fun Maisie."

"You might not blame him, but I do," Hayes muttered, scooping up pulled pork on his fork. "Have you seen him since?"

She pushed the grits around with her plastic fork. "He called a while back. It was actually kind of sweet. I think he felt bad for the way he had acted. Wanted to make sure I was okay."

Hayes's eyes searched hers. "Are you okay?"

Emotion thickened her throat. She pushed past it. "I actually think I am." She hesitated, trying to collect her thoughts, not even really sure herself. "My heart changed with Laurel's murder. I just don't think I ever knew the world could be so cruel. You always hear of bad things happening, but how could something so horrible happen to someone so good?" She glanced to her food, so Hayes wouldn't see the welling of her tears. "It took me a very long time to see the beauty in things again. And to realize that, while there are evil people, there are more good."

A long sigh fell from his lips, and he gave a slow nod. "I can understand that."

She wiped the fallen tear before he noticed. "So, to answer your dating question, I didn't date the year after Laurel left us, because I didn't want anyone in my life."

"What about the year after that?"

She looked at him, finding his attentive stare on her. *I helped you,* she wanted to say. But not wanting to make him feel bad about taking up her time, she said instead, "The brewery started to take off and that took over my life."

He stared at her intently, a million unknowns hanging in the air, and she looked out and found Ralph giving her a cute smile from behind his tent. She smiled back and gave him a little wave. He returned it, but then the smile vanished and he looked away.

One look at Hayes told her why. Hayes glared in the guy's direction. *Don't,* his expression demanded. This time, she smiled. "So, enough about me, you did spend the night in jail. Are you sure you're really okay?"

Hayes looked at her with something that looked like possession flaring in his eyes. "I am now."

7

By the time they got back to their room for the night at the Range, Hayes was almost too spent from the long day to notice the hellish room they'd walked into. *Almost.* What had Clara been thinking when booking this place?

An oil painting of a deer in the forest hung over the queen-size bed with the brown and orange floral bedspread, the same orange color of the shag carpet. While the place itself looked clean enough, Hayes suspected it hadn't been redecorated since the 1970s.

"Yeah, it went really well," Maisie said into her phone to Clara as she shut the door behind her.

Hayes dropped their overnight bags by the end of the bed and then pointed toward the bathroom.

"Shower," he mouthed.

Maisie gave him a thumbs-up and said to Clara, "Right? I was thrilled with how excited everyone seemed to be. My Instagram was blowing up all night." Hayes headed for the bathroom door, but paused before closing it as she added, "Yup, Hayes was fine. Don't worry. We're all good here."

Hayes didn't feel fine at all. He felt fraught with tension when he shut the door, noting the constant dripping coming from the pedestal sink as he ditched his clothes. He imagined all Clara did was worry. All the time. He didn't blame her. She was a single mother, with a world of responsibility on her shoulders. But damn, he wished her sisters could have seen her tonight. The crowd loved her. All that charm, cuteness, and spunk bewitched them.

They hadn't been the only ones. His father's warning weighed heavy on Hayes's mind all night. What the fuck was he doing? He had no business putting his hands on Maisie until his head and heart were right.

Leaving his clothes in a heap on the floor, he turned the water on as hot as he could stand it. The old pipes began creaking and complaining as he stepped into the shower and pulled the clear shower curtain closed. The lack of water pressure didn't bode well, but it would deal with the grime and dirt from the festival, which only added to the stench on him from sitting in a jail cell all night.

He used the shampoo in the little bottle to wash his hair, his mind slowly drifting back to Maisie. His head kept telling him to keep his distance from her, but one look at her tonight and those roadblocks vanished. Her sweet eyes pulling him in, the gorgeous curves of her body moving beneath his hands, her lips that he'd almost believed were handmade for him. He remembered her soft moans from last night, the feel of her tight heat around him. The hot water rushed down his chest to his hard cock and his hand followed. Desperate not to feel pain or heartache, he shut his eyes, leaned his head back into the water, and he grasped his dick and squeezed. Slow. Easy. Tight. Just the way her body had. He groaned as he ran his hand down to the base and then up again.

"You're not having all the fun without me, are you?"

Hayes couldn't find the strength to drop his hand. Fuck no. He stroked himself a little faster as she slipped into the bathroom and slowly removed her clothes before coming into the shower. Her soft blond hair rested along the curves of her breasts, her small dark nipples puckered, begging for his mouth. He fought to find logic. To remember the reason having her again was a bad idea, but he couldn't acknowledge a single thing but the hot raging need burning through him. Still, he shook with the building tension and admitted, "I'm trying very hard not to touch you again."

"Hmmm." She stepped closer, and he slid his hands over her backside as she pressed all of her incredible curves against him. "Does this make it harder not to touch me?"

His cock twitched against her stomach, and he grinned. "It makes something harder."

Her cheeks flushed as she took a step back and licked her lips, taking in his hardened length. The hunger on her face could make him come alone, but there wasn't a chance in hell he'd finish that fast. He needed this. Needed *her.* Her hooded eyes finally lifted to his face again and entranced him as she slowly lowered to her knees, taking his cock in her hands.

"How about now, Hayes?" she rasped, tearing him apart with those beautiful eyes. "Do you want me to touch you?"

He brushed his knuckles against her cheek. "Fuck, yeah."

With the spray of the shower beating at his back, she slowly took him in, dragging her lips across him before she twirled her tongue around the tip. Overwhelmed by the pleasure, he tossed his head back and moaned. The water soaked his face and ran down his chest to where she played, caressing him with long, slow strokes while her mouth followed.

And she didn't stop, not for a second, not until she had him moaning and trembling and about ready to fucking blow.

Only then did she gently drag her teeth along his shaft. He shuddered, and she laughed huskily. "You like that, huh?"

"I like everything you do to me," he growled, and her squeal of laughter echoed in the shower when he gathered her in his arms. He quickly hit the faucet, turning off the shower.

Soaking wet, and not caring, he had them out of the bathroom and back in the bedroom, where he'd noticed she'd already pulled back the bedspread, leaving only the sheets, as well as a condom.

She laughed again when he tossed her onto the bed, tummy down. Staring at her round bottom, her body available to him, he reached for the condom and sheathed himself. He kissed the dimples on her bottom before sliding his tongue up her spine until he reached her neck. "I like you like this." She tilted her head and he nipped her shoulder before running kisses up to her ear. "Waiting for me." He smiled when her fingers dug into the bedsheets. He understood that uncontrollable need. Fuck, he felt it too. Every day for the last few months. Urgent to possess her, he rose enough only to enter her before covering her body with his again. Heat and passion fueled his thrusts, but the friendship between them was how he knew this body, understood her soul. And with every moan she gave, every movement mirrored, meeting him thrust for thrust, they went to a place where no one else could take them. A place that was theirs.

And yet...*and yet*...it still wasn't enough. Needing to get closer, he slid his arms up the bed until he had his fingers threaded with hers. Her breath grew ragged with his hard, slapping thrusts. Wanting more, needing *everything*, he moved harder and faster, skin smacking against skin. Sweat coating his body as the musky scent of their sex infused the air. *Her* scent. Maisie. Her sweet body under his, he squeezed his arms tighter, wanting to shield her from a cruel world. He moved faster, wanting her to get there. Harder. And harder yet. To see her fall apart, let go of everything all because she trusted him.

When she got there, he did too.

He went near cross-eyed as she clamped around him with her climax. Her screams of pleasure taking any control he had left. Only then did he give in to his body's demands and came with a roar and a shudder.

When he finally found the strength to move, he slid off her, onto his back, trying to catch his breath.

"Question," Maisie said, breathless. "Why were you trying not to touch me before?"

Hayes blew out a slow breath and then turned his head, catching her soft, curious eyes. "I don't want to hurt you."

Her smile was slow and totally Maisie. Confident, and a little sassy too. "Nothing about that hurt, Hayes." Her smile fell, brows drew together. "Besides, you couldn't hurt me. I trust you."

He glanced back up to the popcorn ceiling and shut his eyes. The heat left his body in a rush, the silence ripping into him. She was wrong. Hayes *had* hurt her. He broke her world apart, removed a part of her soul.

Hayes couldn't remember the drive to Maisie's house from Denver. Or even knocking on the door very late into the night. He only remembered one thing. The moment the light went out in her eyes. He couldn't even recall what he'd told her, or if he'd been gentle about relaying the message about Laurel's death. He could only watch as her knees took the brunt of her fall, the vomit flew from her mouth, landing in a pile on the hardwood. Hayes went to reach for Maisie, but his feet would not take him there. His soul frozen in such a state, he could not even think of what to do next. The only thing he'd known was he needed to come and tell Maisie what happened to Laurel before she saw the murder on the news.

"No!" she screamed.

Hayes was meant to protect. To defend. He failed Laurel, and he failed Maisie too. Her screams echoed around him, the tears that should rain down his cheeks were stuck somewhere deep inside him.

"Hayes."

Hands suddenly gripped him, shaking him. "What happened?"

He blinked, realizing Clara stood in front of him. "Laurel's dead," he said, but his voice didn't sound like his own.

"No," Maisie screamed again. "No. No. Laurel. No."

Hayes wobbled on his feet, his skin feeling too hot and too cold all at once. But then his gaze fell to the stairs. Clara's son, Mason, stood on the stairs, crying. Clara released Maisie and ran for her son. Slowly, as if time no longer existed, Hayes looked down at Maisie. Amelia hugged her tight, holding her in the way Hayes should have. Laurel would have wanted that. Laurel would be worried about her.

Laurel...

She was gone.

Hayes turned, facing his cruiser, his weapon a heavy weight on his waist. And as he strode into the dark night, he knew Laurel's innocent life wasn't the only one stolen, but part of Maisie's soul, along with his own, died that night too.

"Hayes."

The warmth of Maisie's hand sprawled on his chest brought him back to her. He turned his head again, catching the warm concern in her eyes. Christ, he wanted to believe that this time he'd get everything right, and tell her everything, explain what really happened and why he still struggled. His lips parted and yet, his hot sweat turned ice cold, the words he wanted to say refusing to leave his mouth. "But what if I do hurt you?" he barely managed.

Her hand lay against his heart. "It's incredibly sweet that you're worried about hurting me, but let's focus on the present. We're okay. This is good." She leaned up a little, offering him everything with a single look. "So, tell me, Hayes, what do you want?"

His gaze roamed over her pouty lips, those eyes that pulled him out of the darkness. "You." He moved then, sliding between her legs, putting his weight onto his arms, and dropped his mouth close to hers. "Again, and again, and again, and maybe even then, it won't be enough."

She brushed her lips against his. "Then show me."

And he did. Again, and again, and again.

8

The next morning, the alarm woke Maisie up at eight, but she opted to enjoy the heat and strength of Hayes again before she got into the shower. He'd come in before she got out and kept her busy for another half an hour before they hit the road. They'd grabbed some breakfast burritos and coffee on the way, and she actually felt a little normal in the dream-like haze of the past few days. For months she'd wanted just this, to have something more than friendship with Hayes. And yet, even when she looked over at him, driving with the window down again, the wind in his hair, she could feel him holding back.

The truth was, she wasn't sure he'd ever let go again. Not that she blamed him. He'd been through so much. Too much. Changed in ways that even Maisie wasn't sure she'd ever understand. Hayes had seen Laurel that night. Found her in a way no husband should ever find his wife.

She turned her head, staring out at the trees passing by in a blur, the cars in the double-lane highway rushing past them as Hayes took it easy with the trailer behind his truck.

She racked her brain to figure out how to shake him up a bit, loosen the dust on the way he'd been living. Find a way past those guards around him.

That's when she saw it. First, a giant spinning Ferris wheel. Then the colorful looping roller coaster up ahead.

"Stop," she exclaimed, pointing out the window. "Please, please can we go?"

Hayes glanced out the window then arched an eyebrow at her. "To the amusement park?"

"Yes!" She bounced in her seat, feeling like a kid begging for some candy. It had been years since she'd been to a decent amusement park. For days, she'd been on her best behavior, working hard. A little fun wouldn't hurt anyone. And the truth was, sometimes she wondered if Hayes even remembered how to have fun. She knew for a fact he hadn't been out on the town very much, other than when Beckett dragged him out to the bar for a drink.

Hayes tapped his finger on the steering wheel, his lips thinning. "I hate to sound like an old, crotchety, responsible person, but do we not have another festival to get to?"

"We do," Maisie said slowly. "But Boulder is only an hour away. We've got all day to get there. The festival doesn't start until seven tonight, so we've got time to blow. Come on. It'll be fun." She pressed her hands together on her chest. "Please, please, please."

Hayes shook his head at her then hedged, "Clara can never know about this. I like my balls where they are."

Maisie laughed. "Well, since I like your balls where they are too, I promise she'll never know."

The bright smile he gave her in response stayed with Maisie as they parked the truck. The sweet happiness in that smile stayed with her as Hayes paid for them to get inside the amusement park. The warmth that touched her only grew hotter when she sat next to Hayes as the clanking of the roller-coaster's chain pulled them higher and higher until it began to slow at the top. Laughter and cheering surrounded them, loud music blasting across the blue sky.

She glanced sideways at Hayes when they reached the top and hung there for a second. His easy grin took her breath away.

"Hold on tight," he said, his fingers twined with hers against the bar.

Something broken that lived deep in her chest began to heal, but then the car tipped forward. The wind rushed over her face as the car raced down the metal rails, her scream breaking through the silence as her stomach bottomed out. The *whoosh* of the air brakes forced her head back against the headrest. She burst out laughing and looked over at Hayes, finding his hair wind-blown, a wide smile on his face. The biggest smile she'd seen on him in a very long time.

Feeling like she got today totally right, she hurried out of the roller-coaster car when it pulled to a stop. "Come on," she said, tugging him along. "We only have two hours. I need all the fun."

This was what she could give Hayes that no one else could. She knew how to have fun. *Live. Enjoy. Be free.* She never needed any help with that. And to finally do something that *she* was amazing at, felt good.

Hayes smiled, running a hand through his hair. "Let's do this."

One hour quickly turned into two. They'd gone through a two-story haunted house painted in gloomy colors. She nearly threw up on the swinging pirate ship see-sawing back and forth against a blue sky. And they rode enough roller coasters that the ground felt a little wobbly as she walked toward a funhouse with a creepy clown entrance. She hurried forward, and over her shoulder, she said, "You get a kiss if you find me."

With a chuckle, she rushed inside before he could answer, entering the maze of mirrors. Hands out, Maisie moved along the maze and bumped into more mirrors than she could count, until she was deep enough inside that he couldn't find her too easily. She circled around, only seeing herself. Then she blinked and Hayes stood there, a smile on his face.

She gasped. "How the hell—"

His smile faded to something hotter. He had her up against wall in a millisecond and kissed her with a passion that weakened her knees and had her nearly climbing up his body.

"Get a room," a laughing teenager yelled before he and his group took off running through the maze.

Hayes nipped her bottom lip then chuckled. "We were that stupid once."

"I remember," she said with a laugh. "How did you find me so fast?"

"I followed the floor," he said, gesturing down to the worn hardwood. "This isn't a complicated maze."

She slowly shook her head. "The mirrors always make things so much more confusing. You and your logical brain amaze me."

"Well, you and your creative brain amaze me too." He dropped his chin, the slight scruffiness above his lip tickling hers as he gave her another soft kiss. "I hate to ruin the fun, but we have a schedule we need keep. We should probably get on our way."

She sighed. "Yup, our last festival awaits."

That statement hung in the air between them as they

made their way out of the maze, passing the group of still-laughing teenagers. Maisie tried not to think about what would happen once they got home. Was sex still on the table? Or was this just *fun* while they were away? It didn't feel like only fun, but it also didn't feel like Hayes was offering up much beyond that either. They strode down the row of carnival games, passing by the floating duck game, when Hayes said, "Hold up." He turned to the shooting gallery with pop-up targets, the giant stuffed animals hanging off the ceiling as prizes.

Maisie sidled up to him as he gave the attendant a five-dollar bill. He picked up the gun, took aim. One by one, the targets fell. Maisie had never seen Hayes in action, but she remembered him in his police uniform back in the day. The whole cowboy thing suited him, but he also, with his eyes on the target, looked like a cop.

When the bells dinged to signal the end of the game, the attendant yelled, "We have a winner. Pick a prize."

Hayes glanced back over his shoulder with a shit-eating grin. "Well?"

She studied the stuffed animals around her, trying to find the perfect one to remember this day. Then she found exactly what she was looking for. She pointed. "The bear, please."

The attendant took down the huge bear that was half the size of Maisie and handed it to her. Without looking at them again, the attendant yelled out, "Winner. Winner. Winner. We got ourselves a winner here. Who's next?"

Maisie hugged the bear tight as Hayes asked, "Why the bear?"

"Because it reminds me of you. Of this road trip."

He arched an eyebrow. "I remind you of a bear. Do I want to know why?"

"Oh, it's not so bad." She began walking and he settled into stride with her. "You're all broody and growly, but really, you're all soft and snuggly on the inside."

He snorted. "Please don't repeat that ever."

She laughed and slid her arm through his, inhaling the sweet goodness of the doughnuts sizzling in the vats of oil nearby. "I had no idea you could shoot like that."

"I'm a cop—" He cleared his throat, averting his gaze. "*Was* a cop. Came with the training."

She didn't poke that topic. Hayes was an amazing police officer. He seemed born to protect others. She could tell he missed it, the longing was there is his eyes whenever they talked about his life as a police officer, but she didn't press him on why he'd walked away from his job. She understood the need to let go of an old life to make sure you survived in the new one. They passed a tired toddler crying as his mother tended to the scrape on his knee on the way out the parking lot.

"Ma'am, can I help?" Hayes asked the woman.

She glanced up and gave him a lopsided smile. "I'm all right, but thanks for the offer."

He nodded, striding forward down the rows of parked cars, like his reaction was no big deal.

But it was. To Maisie. She laid her head on his shoulder. "You're sweet, you know that?"

"By offering to help her?" Hayes asked.

"Most people wouldn't do that." Hayes did because he was a public servant. He was born from generations of cops. She dropped a kiss onto his muscled bicep and told him the God's honest truth. "I'm happy you're in my life."

He stopped walking then and pulled her against him, and set those warm whiskey-colored eyes on her. "And I'm happy you're in mine." He kissed her forehead before leveling her with the sweetest smile. "Thank you for today. It's been a long time since..."

She leaned against him and filled in what he couldn't say. "I had a lot of fun too."

His tender smile was his only reply. He turned to walk away, when suddenly, his steps faltered.

"What?" she asked in question, glancing ahead.

She instantly realized the problem. A rush of heat swept over her, and not in a good way. She looked left then right, but only saw cars. She scanned the area again. And again. "Um, Hayes, where is the truck?"

He slowly turned to her, jaw set. "I have no fucking clue."

Hayes swore he'd never step foot into a police station again. Because of Maisie, he'd seen the inside of two in the last two days. He took stock of her sitting in the hallway of the Boulder police department. She kept looking at the clock on the wall, twisting the ring on her finger. Today had been...*amazing*, the best he'd had in a long time. And Maisie was the reason. Something restless in him settled. Something that felt good, instead of painful. Something that told him it wasn't wrong for him to smile.

Needing to be close, he reached over and took her delicate fingers into his, and she jerked her head toward him. "It's going to be okay," he told her.

She gave a quick nod and began fingering her necklace.

Unsure of how to fix this for her, Hayes brushed his thumb across the back of her palm, glancing out at the station. The sound of a crying baby came from the room across the hallway. To his left, officers discussed cases behind glass. To the right, cops were chatting and joking in the breakroom. The camaraderie was something he missed most. After Laurel's murder, he'd shut everyone out. But this place, the smells of old coffee and stale air, felt familiar. Good. Almost like a missing part of Hayes was sitting in there.

Maisie nearly jumped out of her skin when Hayes's cell phone rang. He reached for it in his pocket, looked at the screen. "It's Beckett."

Again, she nodded, not looking at him.

Hayes hit answer and lifted the phone to his ear. "Hey."

"At least this time you're not behind bars," Beckett said by way of greeting.

Hayes snorted, stretching out his legs, keeping Maisie's hand on his thigh. "Hilarious. Care to tell me how you know I'm at a police station?"

At that, Maisie's gaze jerked to him. The remainder of the color left her face, leaving her ghostly white. He made a mental note to find some juice and maybe a chocolate bar after the call, to get her sugar up. He didn't want her passing out or throwing up.

"Your dad called," Beckett replied. "He put me on standby to come and get you guys, since he's stuck at the station, figured you might need a ride."

Hayes called his father on the way to the police station after the cops showed up at the amusement park. He explained the situation, desperate to get more eyes out there looking for his truck and the Three Chicks Brewery trailer. He appreciated his father's kind sentiment. "Thanks for being on standby. We're hanging tight for now. I'll let you know if we need that ride."

Beckett said, "Sounds good. It's un-fucking-real that someone would take the truck at a beer festival. Pretty ballsy. The place had to be packed."

Hayes shifted in his seat, his chest tightening as the guilt of their reality washed over him. "We were at an amusement park on the way to Boulder this morning. It happened there."

A pause. Then Beckett chuckled. "Well, I'm glad to hear that Maisie is rubbing off on you. I don't think I've seen you do anything spontaneous or fun in a long time." Another hesitation, then Hayes chuckled lightly, acknowledging the truth in the statement, as Beckett added, "But, man, I'm sorry this happened. Shitty deal."

"Yeah, thanks," Hayes agreed.

Two male officers, with fresh steaming coffee cups walked by, the keys on their belts jingling, when Beckett asked, "How's Maisie holding up?"

Hayes slid his gaze to her. Her knee bounced a mile a minute, the nail on her thumb bit down to nothing.

"Hanging in there." He scrubbed at his face, rubbing his tired eyes. "I'm hoping this gets wrapped up soon. My dad made some calls to a few sheriffs. They've got units looking for my truck, and the detective working the case seems on top of it."

"That's good. What time do you have to get to Boulder for the festival?"

"Five, at the latest." Hayes looked at the clock on the wall. They still had three hours to find the truck and the trailer. When Maisie's knee began bouncing faster, he squeezed her hand tight, continuing to brush his thumb across her soft skin. "We've got time," he said to reassure her.

Beckett's heavy voice showed his doubts. "What chance do you really think you'll make it to the festival?" When Hayes didn't answer, Beckett snorted. "That bad, eh?"

"Yeah." At this point, there was a fifty-fifty chance

they'd find his truck in time, but Hayes knew the mind of a criminal. They wanted the beer. They'd likely stolen the truck and trailer simply for that. Clara and Amelia could always drive more beer up for the festival, if they found the trailer with the jockey box, but Hayes wasn't sure they'd have the time to pull that off. And of course, there was the other fifty percent chance that they wouldn't find the truck at all.

Beckett asked, "They've got no leads whatsoever?"

"None that the detective working the case knows about, but from what I hear, this isn't the first time a car has gone missing from the amusement park over the last few weeks."

"Pricks," Beckett muttered.

Hayes nearly responded when he noticed a man coming down the hallway. "Listen, I've got to run. I'll reach out if we need that ride."

"Good luck."

The call ended, and Hayes nudged Maisie's arm. "I suspect we've got news."

She glanced to her left and stiffened enough that Hayes held her hand tighter.

Detective Stewart, an older gentleman who was likely not far off from retirement strode toward them. He was a fit guy, obviously lifted weights to keep in shape. His bushy salt-and-pepper beard matched the stylish cut of hair on his head. When they'd first been introduced, he'd worn a three-piece suit. Now his white dress shirt was rolled up at the sleeves. The firm set of his mouth wasn't a good sign.

"We've found your truck and trailer," the detective said, stopping next to Maisie.

She rose on shaky legs. Hayes followed suit, sliding an arm around her back, bringing her close, as she asked, "Where?"

Detective Stewart said, "In a rural area, about five miles from here."

"Thank God," Maisie breathed. "Can we go get it?"

The detective shifted on his feet as he lifted his phone and unlocked it. "I'm afraid I've got some bad news on that front."

He handed Maisie the phone. She narrowed her eyes on the screen, and Hayes leaned in, realizing exactly what he saw. Maisie, with an untrained eye for examining burnt metal, asked, "What exactly am I looking at?"

Detective Stewart said, "Your trailer, I'm afraid. That's all that's left of it."

Maisie's shoulders curled forward, caving into her chest.

The detective added to Hayes, "Your truck is the next photo. It's no better. They were found at a local junkyard."

With a shaky hand, Maisie lifted the phone to Hayes for him to look. Hayes handed it back to the detective, not caring about his goddamn truck at the moment. He gathered a trembling Maisie into his arms. His vision tunneled. "Thank you for the update," Hayes said to the detective. "Can you give us a few minutes?"

"Of course," the detective said with a soft, sad smile and then strode away.

Maisie's fingers locked onto Hayes's T-shirt. "That's it. It's over. I failed." Her voice was quiet, too quiet. Her complexion sickly. "All because I decided we needed fun. I fucked this up, like I always do. Clara and Amelia will never forgive me."

"They will forgive you," Hayes countered. "They love you, and this was absolutely not your fault."

No, this was his fault. He should have kept them on track for the event. That was his fucking job. Maisie needed his stability. That's why he was there with her, even if she never outright said it. Hayes understood pure rage. He'd tasted the bitterness of it for years, and that same dark ugliness flickered through him again. "It's going to be all right." His chin rested on top of her head, the image of the burnt-out trailer filling his mind. "We'll figure this out."

"There's nothing to figure out," she said harshly, and met him with a hard stare. "It's done. It's over. Please call Beckett to come get us." The coldness of her voice hit him before she strode away with heavy steps.

Hayes reeled from the shadows in her eyes. The lack of life there. The brightness that those criminals stole away.

Someone would pay.

9

The farmhouse had always been Maisie's favorite place, the one spot where nothing could ever touch her, where everything felt safe. Until tonight. Clara and Amelia sat around the kitchen table in their pajamas, hair up in matching messy buns. For as long as Maisie could remember, she'd always been the outsider, the one different from her sisters. When they shopped together, Maisie painted. When they watched chick flicks, Maisie snuggled up with a good book. After Laurel, she felt that gap between her and her sisters close. But now, she felt a world away from them again. The silent heaviness in the room made each breath that passed through Maisie's lips feel more and more strangled. The only light came from the hanging fixture above the kitchen table. Upstairs, Mason had been asleep for hours, the steady clicking of the grandfather clock in the hallway a constant *tick* grating on Maisie's last nerve.

After Beckett had picked them up at the police station, the drive home had been equally as silent. The only words exchanged had been when Hayes walked her to her front door, took her in his arms and hugged her tight. "I'll call you tomorrow," he said.

When Maisie walked through her front door, she met Clara's frown and Amelia's sad eyes.

Both remained looking that way as they sat across from her at the table. When the silence became daunting, Maisie played with the dried, crispy leaves of wilting flowers in the vase. The dead leaves crumbled between her fingers. Her heart felt just like that. "I'm sorry."

"This isn't your fault," Amelia said softly, taking Maisie's hand across the table.

"Then why does it feel like it is?" Maisie stared at the crystal vase, unable to face the disappointment in Clara's eyes. She reached for another leaf. It fell apart in her fingers. "Hayes and I were doing so well. And, because, on a whim, I wanted some fun, I cost us this last festival." She slid her fingers over another leaf.

"Please stop killing the flower," Clara said. "It did nothing to you." The softness in Clara's voice made Maisie lift her gaze. Clara smiled gently at her, making Maisie fight back tears. "You tried your best. We both know that."

Amelia agreed with a nod. "We do."

Maisie didn't feel better. If anything, she felt worse. They'd worked so hard. Done everything right. Maisie, no matter what she did, always messed things up.

Whatever showed on Maisie's expression made Clara shake her head slowly. "I honestly don't understand how so many bad things can happen to one person. It's like you've been hexed or something."

It had truly begun to feel that way. "You know, maybe that is what's going on here. Maybe someone hates me and has hexed me into failing. All the time."

Amelia said, "Who would hate you, Maisie-Moo?"

"If you find out, let me know," Maisie said.

Amelia snorted a laugh.

Maisie pulled her hands away and pressed the bottom of her palms into her eyes. "Seriously, though, what are we going to do now? We needed that festival, right?"

"We did, yes," Clara answered. "But there's not much we can do about that. The only thing we can do is wait until the insurance money comes in so we can repurchase what we need for future festivals. There are a few more coming up in a couple of months we could hit. They're not as big as these last few, but it's still something."

Amelia asked, "How long do you think it will take to get the insurance money?"

"I don't know," Clara said grimly.

Maisie considered, facing the daunting reality. "But can we still get a distributor without that last festival? Or will another brewery stand out above us?"

Clara shrugged. "I don't know that either."

That was never a good sign. Clara always had ideas and answers. Maisie's throat tightened, and she dropped her head against the table, hard enough it hurt. "I hate this fucking curse on me."

Silence descended, even heavier than before.

Until Amelia said, "Do you remember when you broke Nan's special mug?"

"Yes," Maisie said into the table, banging her head once more. How could she forget that horrible memory? Their grandmother drank her tea out of the same fine china glass for as long as Maisie could remember. A year after their grandmother passed away, Maisie had been looking at the mug. It'd slipped from her hand and the mug smashed to pieces. Maisie remembered her tears.

"Do you remember what Pops said to you?"

"No," she grumbled.

Hands gripped Maisie's head, forcing her gaze up. Clara's eyes were untypically soft. "He said that things break, fall apart in ways you may never expect."

Amelia nodded, a knowing look on her face. She left the kitchen and returned a moment later with a picture frame. In that frame was a mosaic that Maisie had made of the glass shards. Amelia placed it on the table in front of Maisie and said, "You were really young at the time, so I don't think you could have understood how happy Pops was that you made this."

Maisie slid her fingers over the glass. The work was messy, glue visible, but Pops had framed it.

Clara asked, "Do you remember what he said to you after you gave him this?"

"Not exactly," Maisie said, trying to recall. "I remember his smile."

Clara's eyes went distant, lost in a memory before she blinked, clearing them. "He told you no one was like you. That most people would have thrown the mug out. But you looked at something broken and made it beautiful. That was your gift to the world."

Emotion clogged Maisie's throat and she choked on a sob. "I miss him."

Both of her sisters nodded in understanding, tears in their eyes. The world was a better place with Pops. Pops had a special kind of love. Maisie missed that love. Love where she felt wholly understood.

In the quiet space of the moment, she realized she felt that with Hayes too. He only seemed to see the good, even if the bad was undeniably obvious. But she could feel him holding back, and right to the heart of it, she knew there was a good chance he'd never let his guard down. Not completely anyway. Not enough.

"I guess what I'm trying to say here," Amelia said, "is while this seems really bad right now, I'd like to think that Pops was right. Maybe all of this is happening for a reason because something bigger and better will work out. I mean, it has to, right?"

Always the optimist. That was Amelia. Maisie couldn't afford that luxury. "No, it doesn't have to work out. It never does."

Amelia frowned.

Clara drew in a deep breath and rubbed her eyes. Ignoring what Maisie said, she pressed on, "We've got to figure out a plan."

She meant *she* had to figure out a plan. Maisie clearly wasn't going to be the one to fix all this.

Amelia agreed with a nod and then said to Maisie, "You did really well on those first two festivals. It *could* be enough. Especially if we get some awards too. We just won't know until all of that comes in."

Maisie felt the ground slowly dropping out from under her. She hadn't wanted this. She wanted to do her part. Be one of the reasons the brewery became a success. To actually finish something she started. To come out on top.

Clara rose from her chair, pushing it back under the table. "We'll just have to take this day by day. Let's get some sleep. We can talk more in the morning."

Maisie stayed put, resting her hand in her chin. "I'll be right behind you." First, she needed to wallow with a bag chips.

"Okay," Clara said, then gave a soft smile. "Please leave us some of the chips."

Maisie snorted. "I wasn't—"

Clara lifted her eyebrows.

"Fine," Maisie hedged, "I'm totally eating all the chips because I need to eat my emotions. I'll buy more tomorrow."

Clara smiled, moved in close and kissed Maisie's cheek. "Good night."

"Night."

Once Clara strode off, Amelia took Maisie into one of her warm hugs. "It's all going to be okay, Maisie-Moo. Promise. You'll see."

Maisie highly doubted that but kept the thought to herself as Amelia smiled. "Besides, the good thing here—"

Maisie lifted her brows. "There is a good thing that happened tonight?"

Amelia gave a crooked smile and an easy shrug. "The worst has already happened. What more could go wrong?"

A loud *thump* banged against the window. The sound they'd heard many times over the years in this house. A bird hitting the window hard enough to kill itself. Maisie sighed and gave Amelia a knowing look. "Great. Now I'm killing things."

Amelia cringed. "Okay, *that* is the worst thing. What else—"

"Don't say it," Maisie cut in. "Just don't. We both know that when I'm involved, anything and everything can go wrong."

Amelia didn't respond to that. She just did what she did best, threw her arms around Maisie tight. "Don't stay up too late." She grabbed the bag of ketchup-flavored chips and tossed them at Maisie before she blew her a kiss. "Night, night."

Maisie ripped open the bag and shoved a handful into her mouth. "Night."

Between the crunching sounds, she heard little footsteps. A quick look behind her had her smiling. "You're supposed to be in bed," she told Mason.

"I'm not sleepy," he told her. "And you have chips."

"Chips for me," she said firmly. "Your mother will kill me. Get that cute butt back up to bed."

He turned and wiggled that cute butt at her then ran toward her, jumping onto her lap. "Please, Auntie Maisie, I won't tell. I'm so, so hungry."

She frowned at all that sweetness coming her way. "You know that I am the expert at giving puppy-dog eyes."

"That's because we're alike," he said with a big grin. "That's what mama always says."

Maisie kissed his cheek. "That's because we're awesome, and awesome people should eat all the chips." She turned the open bag to him. "If your mother asks, this never happened."

He shoved a hand into the bag and chomped away. "Deal."

Across town, Beckett pulled his dark gray Ford F-350 Super Duty to a stop outside the police station after they'd dropped off Maisie at home. The River Rock Police Station had moved into the old courthouse on Main Street long before Hayes had worked there. The skies had opened twenty minutes ago, a downpour settling over the town, bringing sheets of rain from the west. Beckett's headlights caught the droplets, the windshield wipers set to high, unable to keep up with the hammering of the rain.

The front door was right there, and Hayes fought against his churning stomach at the thought of walking through the doors.

Obviously sensing his hesitation, Beckett said, "I can take you home. It's been a long day. Why don't you sleep on this?"

Hayes glanced at his lifelong friend. The only man he'd ever admit his weaknesses to. "I did this to Maisie. I need to fix it."

Beckett threw the truck into park. "Oh, yeah, you stole your own truck and set it on fire?"

Hayes snorted. "I should never have agreed to stop at that damn amusement park."

"That's idiotic," Beckett spat. "For one, you sounded fucking happy when I called. Second, you had no idea that stopping there would lead to someone stealing your truck and Maisie's trailer."

Hayes thrust his hand in his hair, the truck feeling a little too hot for his liking. A little too small even. "I should have kept us on track. You didn't see her." His chest tightened, and he blew out a harsh breath to ease the tension. "She needed this win. To do this for her grandfather. The blow of the failure—"

Beckett gave a dry laugh.

Hayes snarled in Beckett's direction. "This is funny to you?"

"Funny?" Beckett hummed the word like he was tasting it on his tongue. "No, it's too fucking sad to be funny. How about we stop playing this game where you're helping her because of any other reason than you care about her."

"I do care about her," Hayes said in an instant.

Beckett gave a knowing look. "You want me to say how much you care about her?"

Hayes's gaze cut to the rain droplets in the headlights. *You love her* echoed in the truck between them.

Beckett added, "For the life of me, I can't figure out why the hell you're dancing around that fact."

Hayes swallowed the thick lump in his throat. Lost in the rain beating the windshield, he forced the words out. "What if I get this all wrong? Fuck this up and hurt her."

Beckett hesitated. "Ah."

He knew how broken Hayes was. A few days after the murder, Beckett had pulled Hayes's drunk ass out of a bar. In his drunken stupor, he'd cried the truth to Beckett, sobbed in a way Hayes didn't know himself capable of sobbing, that he'd failed to protect his wife and put a bull's-eye on her back. Hayes listened to the steady rhythmic beating of the rain and admitted something he never thought he would. "I can't..." *Lose her* got caught in his throat.

Beckett drew in a deep breath and blew it out slowly. "Listen, man, Maisie's got a big, loving heart. Don't hide from her. She's got hard love for you, my friend. Either talk to her, tell her everything, and see how it plays out, or don't, but dancing around this is going to hurt her more than telling her the truth." He cupped Hayes's shoulder. "It's been a long time, buddy. It's time to move on from this."

Hayes bowed his head and nodded. Unsure what to add beyond that, he said, "Thanks for picking us up."

"Of course," Beckett said.

Hayes opened the door then and stepped out in the pouring rain.

"Hayes," Beckett called. He turned back, the warm rain battering his face. Beckett gave a soft smile. "Tell Maisie you came here tonight to fix this for her."

"Why?" The warm water dripped off Hayes's nose.

"Just tell her."

Beckett slowly drove off as Hayes slammed the door

shut. He watched the headlights fade into the darkness before he turned toward the station. His gut twisted. This time, he pushed that weakness aside. He'd come for a reason, and he couldn't run, not anymore. He'd failed to protect Laurel. He would not fail Maisie. He blew his drenched hair out of his face and trotted up the stairs, entering the station quickly, wiping his boots on the mat.

The space was modernized with the reception desk at the front near the waiting room. A hallway down the left side led to a larger room with beehive desks, some with computers on top.

The night shift receptionist noticed him, and her eyes widened. "Hayes. This is an unexpected surprise. It's so good to see you."

"Hi, Phillis," Hayes said with a smile. She was in her sixties, with black dyed hair and bright red nail polish on fake nails, a face full of wrinkles from heavy smoking, and a love of fine whiskey. "You've been well?"

"Same old, same old around here," she said. "Are you here to see your father?"

Hayes nodded, giving his hair a shake, removing some of the water. "I am. Is he in his office?"

"Sure is." She buzzed the door next to her desk. "Go on back."

"Thanks." He strode through, the door quickly locking behind him. Each step took all of his strength; with each one, he was desperate to turn around and go the other way. He had decided to transfer to Denver to stand on his own two feet, without having his father watching his every move. And in the years since he'd last been here, not much had changed. He passed the water fountain, then the waiting room where a couple of teenagers lingered, and officers sat at their cubicles doing desk work. Filing cabinets opening and closing, police radios squawking, every sound was exactly the same. It felt like no time had passed at all.

When he finally reached the corner office and saw his father behind his desk, Hayes asked, "Big case?"

Dad's head jerked up, his eyes bulging before his expression went into cop mode, completely blank and unreadable. "I see you got home safely, minus a truck."

Hayes nodded, entered the office, and sat in the guest chair. "I'll miss that truck."

"I bet," Dad agreed. Then he gestured at the papers on his desk. "We're down a couple of officers, I'm trudging through applicants for a handful of positions." Which explained why his father had pressured Hayes about getting back on the force. His dad tilted his head to the side, laced his fingers together on top of his desk. "Now, let's get to the reason why you're here." *Because I never thought you'd step foot in here again,* his focused gaze suggested.

A telephone rang out in the cubicles, fingers tapped constantly against keyboards. Hayes shut it all out with a steady breath. "I want to investigate who stole my truck and Maisie's trailer."

His father replied, "Boulder's working that case. And need I remind you that you're not a cop anymore? Your choice, not mine."

Hayes dealt with the first part of his rebuttal. "The case could be worked in conjunction with River Rock, if the request came in from the chief of police."

Dad leaned back in his chair. His slow smile began to build. "Ah, which brings us back to the second part of my statement."

Hayes nodded. "What are you asking from me?"

"Six months. Work this case, then work here for me. If

you want to walk away after that, then walk. But I want six months of your service."

Hayes knew why. His father thought he'd miss the job, realize that the law was in his blood. It had been a part of him. Maybe the best parts of him. At the moment, Hayes didn't care if that love came back. For Maisie, he needed to right this wrong. Hayes rose. "How long will it take you to reinstate me?"

"Officially, about a week," his father said, his body posture perking up. "Unofficially, you can start tomorrow morning." Dad hesitated now. The look in his eye was not that of the police chief, but of Hayes's father. Attentive. Concerned. "Before we move ahead with this, do you have your mind straight? I do not need you becoming a liability."

The light draining from Maisie's eyes when she saw the burnt-out trailer filled Hayes's mind. He'd seen the light go out of her eyes before. Never fucking again. He tapped his knuckles against the top of the chair. "Yes. Make it happen." And with every step out of the station, he wasn't thinking about his regrets or concerns, he only thought of Maisie.

10

The night seemed to drag on and on and on, and Maisie had tossed and turned the majority of it, mulling over the entire situation. All she wanted was to fulfill Pops's final wishes, but all she did was fail. And late into the night, as Maisie stared at the bright moon outside her window, she couldn't shake the feeling that Clara was right. She'd caught a curse somewhere in her life. Maisie had no idea by who or what, but the more she thought on it, the more she wondered why, no matter how hard she tried, everything went wrong. What had she done to irritate fate?

When exhaustion finally swallowed her up, Maisie dreamed of fairies with magical powers and pretty meadows with vivid, bright colors. When she awoke to a beautifully sunny day, she knew exactly what she needed to do. Extreme times called for extreme measures, and she was done sitting around waiting to fail again. She snatched her phone off her bedside table and dialed Penelope.

A sleepy Penelope answered the phone. "What's wrong?"

"I have to go see Luna Whittle," Maisie said, staring up at the flower shaped medallion above her ceiling fan.

Penelope croaked, "The psychic?"

"Yes!"

Shuffling sounds filled the phone line, and then Penelope groaned. "Maisie, it's seven o'clock in the morning."

"I know. I'm sorry for calling so early, but please tell me you'll come with me."

"Of course, I'll come with you," Penelope responded immediately. Some of the sleepiness left Penelope's voice. "What time do you need me ready by?"

Maisie blew out a relieved breath. "I'll text you once I know. Thank you. You have no idea how much I appreciate this."

"You don't need to thank me," Penelope said, warmth enveloping her voice. "You'd do the same thing for me. See you soon. Bye."

"Bye." Maisie ended the call, sat up, and leaned against the wall of pillows behind her. Penelope was probably the only one who wouldn't judge Maisie for taking a wild next step.

Determined to get her life back on track, Maisie opened her web browser on her phone, pulling up Luna's website. Using the online booking system, she selected the only available appointment for nine thirty and settled back into bed with her phone on her chest.

Something good would come out of this. She wasn't sure how she knew that with such certainty, but she felt it bone deep. She'd gone to high school with Luna, and rumors said she'd come from generations of psychics and mediums. Maisie didn't know what to believe, but doing things the normal way was getting her nowhere, and if there was a hex on her, she wanted it off. Pronto.

Going back to sleep was impossible. Maisie decided to deal with the laundry from the road trip. She showered and shaved, spending a little more time than normal, just in case she saw Hayes later. She dressed in a floral print baby doll dress and paired it with strappy sandals, leaving her hair down and letting the natural wave take over, and added light makeup.

Before she knew it, nine o'clock arrived, and she was on the way to pick up Penelope. She opened the roof of her MINI convertible, letting the warm sun give her the big dose of vitamin D she needed. When she arrived at the two-story house Penelope shared with Darryl, Penelope was already waiting outside on the porch. She wore jean shorts and a pretty, flowy tank top, her long dark hair was in a messy bun, and fresh makeup on her face. While Maisie was close with her sisters, she'd been on the same wavelength as Penelope since birth, and Penelope's sweet smile when Maisie pulled into the driveway loosened the tension in Maisie's chest.

While Maisie had become closer to Clara and Amelia since Laurel's death, they would never understand Maisie the way Penelope did. They'd question her sanity or try to talk her out of letting a psychic solve her problems, but the only thing Penelope said after the getting into the car was, "All right, you big nut ball, what are we asking Luna today?"

Maisie hit the road again. "I take it you've heard what happened to Hayes's truck and my trailer, right?"

The strands of Penelope's hair blew in the wind. She laughed and grabbed her hair at the base of her neck. "Maisie, we live in a small town. Everyone has heard what happened."

"Right," Maisie muttered, swallowing back the bile in her throat. Of course, everyone knew she'd failed. *Again.*

"Well, here's the thing. I've always just gone with the flow and accepted that life is just a big cesspool of disappointments, but I need answers now. Luna will give me those."

"Okay then," Penelope said, as if that explained everything. "So, how was the sex with Hayes?"

Maisie swerved on the road, her tire hitting the curb before she righted the car. "Please tell me that is *not* running along the gossip train?"

"Ha! I knew it. You totally slept with him." Penelope nudged Maisie's arm with a playful shove, crossing her legs. "Tell me everything. Leave no detail out. I want all the juice."

Maisie had planned to tell her already. She heard the dreaminess in her own sigh. "The sex...God, Penelope, the sex was out of this world."

"Not surprised," Penelope said with a waggle of her eyebrows and a shit-eating grin. "Hayes is all broody and rough, a total man."

Train track lights flashed up ahead. Maisie slowed the car to a stop and put it in park as the gates lowered, blocking off the road as the train suddenly flew by. "I actually think being with him was even better than I could have imagined. There's just so much..."

"Passion? Tension? Chemistry?"

Maisie nodded. "Yeah, all that. But there's more, like, I know Hayes. Really know him. It makes the whole experience just different, I guess."

"Because of what you've been through together?"

"That," Maisie agreed with another nod, "and that we've seen each other at our best and at our very worst. It's like having a best friend who knows every single thing you've ever been through, but then somehow ignites explosive passion too, because they know you enough to do that. I've never had sex like that."

"That's the good stuff," Penelope said. "The everlasting stuff."

Maisie's heart squeezed in agreement. "Tell that to Hayes for me, would ya?" she joked, placing her foot back on the brake and shifting into drive as the train finally vanished and the gates lifted again.

As the car bounced over the tracks, Penelope asked, "Do I want to know what that even means?"

"It means I'm still not sure where things are going with us," Maisie explained with a sigh. Penelope knew everything. Maisie leaned on her when Laurel passed away. She told Penelope when she started developing feelings for Hayes. "And isn't that weird? I mean, I don't really get the feeling that he's holding back because I'm Laurel's best friend; this is something different."

"Hmm," Penelope hummed. "He won't talk to you about what's going on?"

"I haven't really asked," Maisie admitted. "And yes, I'm know that's because I'm scared if I ask, then he'll shut me out."

Penelope gave a dry laugh. "Okay, then I won't say that, because you have your answer. You just have to talk to him."

Seemed so easy, but it wasn't at all. Hayes had been through a lot. Too much. He finally seemed happy again, she didn't want to push him too fast, too soon. Maisie stayed lost in that thought for the last few minutes of the drive. When they reached downtown, people were already walking the streets, visiting the farmer's market, and shopping in the quaint stores. She pulled to a stop next to the red brick storefront with the black awning next to an old book-

store. The hanging wooden sign read: LUNA WHITTLE.
HOUSE OF MAGIC.

"Ready?" Penelope asked, undoing her seat belt.

Maisie stared at the sign. She needed to get answers. For
everything. "Hell yes," she told Penelope and then got out in
an instant. She strode toward the small store, with Penelope
hot on her heels.

When she entered, ethereal music played through the
speaker on the desk. A black cat with bright green eyes
cleaned its paw on the counter. Strings of lights hung
around the ceiling, with plants decorating the corners of the
room. Along the far wall were shelves displaying tea sets
and herbal teas, with celestial pictures on any available
surface. Scented candles warmed the space, smelling both
earthy and spicy.

The cat meowed, almost in greeting, when Luna came
out from the private room at the back. She was everything
one would expect a psychic to look like. She had long blond
hair that was the whitest blond Maisie had ever seen. Her
eyes were a striking gray color that stayed with a person
after they peered into them. Luna was both soft and sweet,
and full of so much warm light, it practically exploded out
of her.

"Hi, Maisie," Luna said with a bright smile. "It's so nice
to see you."

"Good to see you too," Maisie said, stepping farther into
the shop. "Have you met my cousin Penelope?"

"Not yet, but I did sense you when you moved to town."
Luna smiled.

Penelope laughed nervously, settled in next to Maisie,
and grinned down at the cat, giving him scratches on the top
of his soft, furry head. "Oh, you are such a lover."

"He most definitely is," Luna said. "Please feel free to sit and relax while Maisie and I chat."

"Thanks." Penelope sidled up to Maisie. "I think I'll just visit with this sweet fluff ball while you're having your talk."

"Oh, yes," Luna said. "He will like that very much."

Feeling oddly nervous, Maisie gave Penelope a quick wave and then followed Luna into the private room. Curtains draped from the ceiling to the floor. A round table with a fringed cloth sat in the center of the room, with two cushioned chairs around the table. In the middle of the table were crystals in a bowl.

"Please, take a seat," Luna said.

Maisie did as she asked, wiping her sweaty palms on her dress.

Luna sat across from her, reaching her hands out, palms up. "Please give me your hands."

Maisie exhaled slowly and slid her hands into Luna's delicate ones. For as long as she'd known Luna, she'd never had a reading done by her. She never really believed in it all. But the way Maisie had gone about things wasn't working anymore. She needed a way out. And people in town swore by Luna's gifts. Besides, Clara had planted the idea with her hex talk; Maisie was simply running with it.

Luna's head cocked, wise eyes warm. "Is there something specific you'd like to address?"

"I think I might be hexed," Maisie admitted. "Can you tell if I am?"

"I can try." Luna bowed her head, breathed deep. Once. Twice. And again. "Ah, I see," she finally said, lifting her bright gaze. "No, you're not hexed. You're simply not doing what you should be doing. And your guardian angel, which I like to call your guide, is annoyed that you're not listening."

Maisie had heard Luna was amazing, but that came out

so fast and clear that Maisie's mouth dropped open. "Okay, so how exactly do I fix all this?"

"You've got to start listening to your guide," Luna explained, as if that was all very simple. "Your chance for happiness is coming to a head. Your guide is trying very hard to get you to hear the message—you need to stop and listen." She cocked her head, eyes closed, a look of such peace crossing her face. "The message I keep hearing is that to succeed, you need to be yourself. Trust in your heart."

"All right," she said, feeling like she hadn't trusted in her heart for a very long time. Since the brewery opened, she'd been following Clara and Amelia's leads.

Luna opened her eyes, a twinkle in their depths, and she gave a nod like she already figured Maisie out. "Once you accept your place in this world, things will become less hard for you. Life will settle into where it should be, and your guide will quiet down." She hesitated, her head tilting again. "I see a man."

Maisie stiffened. "A man."

"Yes," Luna said slowly, glancing back down at Maisie's palm. "A man you care for very deeply. Your souls are twined intimately in ways most are not. But this man, he's got a secret. A deep one that still wounds him."

The direction change made Maisie's head spin. "Do you know what kind of secret?" she all but whispered.

Luna snapped her eyes to Maisie's again, and rose, the color in her face oddly gone. "I'm afraid that truth is not mine to share. That's all I have for you today. If things don't settle for you in a week, come back, and I'll see what I can do to ease this guide of yours."

Maisie rose on shaky legs. She took a step forward to leave, when something suddenly occurred to her. "Do you know who my guide is?" she asked.

Luna gave a gentle smile. "Your Pops, of course." As Maisie reeled from that, Luna said, "And, Maisie? Ask for help. It's out there."

The sun began to set over the mountains outside of Hayes's office window. He'd spent the last few hours going through the surveillance footage from various cameras at the amusement park hoping he could catch a glimpse of the truck leaving. Hayes had watched the footage again...and again...and again. They didn't have a direct shot of the parking lot where the truck was parked. So far, he'd come up empty. Last night, he'd crashed at home after a hot shower, only to come back into the station at eight o'clock this morning after word came in that Detective Stewart agreed to work a joint investigation. Since then, he hadn't left his chair except to grab food. And Hayes felt each and every hour that had followed. His eyes strained, but his gut told him there was something in these videos he could use to catch the person who hurt Maisie. Exhausted, he stretched out his shoulders and leaned back against his chair, rubbing his eyes.

The phone on the desk rang. "Taylor," he said by way of greeting.

"Detective Stewart calling from Boulder," he said, and after a short pause, he added, "Neil for short." He chuckled.

"Hey, Neil," Hayes said. "Hayes here. What can I do for you?"

"Hayes, glad to work this case alongside you," Neil said. "I'm reaching out to see if you've gotten anywhere on your end."

Hayes glanced at the report he'd printed off this

morning after the detective had shared the online file. "At the moment, nothing is jumping out at me."

Neil made a low noise in his throat. "I'm in the same boat over here. I've interviewed the three people on the suspects' list I sent you but have ruled them all out."

"Good to know." Hayes tucked the phone between his shoulder and ear. He grabbed that list and scratched out the names, frustrated he didn't have any names of his own to add to that list. "Any other updates?"

"Prints didn't turn up anything in the databases. Not that there were that many to begin with. The fire damage, as you saw, was excessive."

Hayes grabbed the copied photograph of his truck beneath the pile of papers. He loved that truck, but there wasn't much of it left. A total write-off. He'd got the insurance claim rolling on that this morning. Then he reached for the photograph of Maisie's trailer. Burned beyond recognition. "You'll keep me in the loop if anything develops there."

"Of course. Call too, if you see anything I'm not."

"Will do."

"I'm heading home for the night, but I'll be back in at eight tomorrow morning."

"Same here. Hopefully, with fresh eyes."

"Agreed. Have a good night."

"You too."

The line went dead. Hayes returned the phone to its base and then rubbed the back of his neck, wishing the answer popped out at him. He wanted to get this solved for Maisie. He needed her to know he'd caught the bastards who'd cut her so deeply.

Laughter coming from the hallway made him lift his head. Three guys strode by, a blur of blue uniforms and weapons, but then suddenly one of those men froze. Hayes chuckled now, as wide eyes greeted him.

"Hey," Hayes said.

Darryl entered the doorway, his stare incredulous. "All right, I know it's been a shitty, long day, but you are sitting there, right?"

"As far as I know, yes." Hayes laughed.

Darryl gave a flick of his chin at the two guys with him. Cops that Hayes had never met, obviously rookies, seeing as they both looked young. Once they continued on down the hallway to the locker room, Darryl leaned against the door-jamb, arms folded. "Something bad must have happened to have you sitting behind a desk with a case in front of you. What's going on?"

Hayes leaned back against his chair, lacing his hands together behind his head. "Did you hear about my truck and Maisie's trailer?"

Darryl's mouth twitched. "Ah, so she's the reason you finally gave in to your father."

Hayes snorted and avoided that line of conversation. Instead, he said, "No one was going to work her case, but me."

Darryl's head cocked at the statement Hayes made. He finally nodded his understanding and asked, "Have you told Nash?"

"Not yet," Hayes said, not looking forward to that particular phone call. "I'll be reaching out soon, but I'm hoping we can work something out to keep me on when he needs me." He enjoyed the rush and his friendships at the farm. Though, this time, the thought of getting near a dangerous horse, of hurting himself, which would in turn hurt Maisie, made him pause. Those pained eyes of hers were all he could see. "We'll figure it out," he finished.

"I'm sure you will." Darryl smiled. "Well, buddy, it's damn good to have you here. Are you here to stay?"

Hayes glanced down at the case on the desk. Today, when he'd worked the case, for the first time in years he'd felt...normal. Like he'd come home, and he didn't know how to process that. "I've promised my father six months."

"Good." Darryl smacked a hand against the door. "I'm overrun with rookies. It'll be good to have some backup."

Hayes's mouth twitched. "That sounds irritating."

"Worse than you can even imagine," Darryl drawled, and moved away from the door.

Hayes began cleaning up the papers on his desk. He'd thought Darryl left, but his warm voice jerked Hayes's gaze back to the doorway. "It is good, you know. You being back on the force. This is where you belong."

Not having the words to respond, Hayes nodded.

After Darryl left, Hayes picked up the photograph of Maisie's burnt-out trailer. She always kept directing his life, in good ways, and by all appearances, she didn't even try. From day one, she'd always been there, guiding his hand. First, when he began dating Laurel. Laurel always made time for Maisie, no matter what happened. Hayes had never minded. Their friendship had been a beautiful thing. And he'd overheard Maisie singing Hayes's praises about him being a good husband. When Laurel passed away, Maisie had been there to scrape him up off the floor, regardless of that fact that she'd been hurting too. She'd pushed on, showing him the beauty in the world, when he couldn't see it at all. She gave him reasons to smile and laugh.

He missed her. His head told him to take a break, let this thing between them breathe a little.

His heart... *Fuck.* He grabbed his phone off his desk and texted her: Busy tonight?

Her response was immediate. Depends?

On?

If I'm getting busy with you.

He chuckled, heat flooding him, just that easily. He was sure she had no idea the power she could wield over him if she wanted. Since I can't seem to refuse you anything, that's very likely.

Good. Come meet me at the brewery. I'm in the barn.

See you in 20.

He gathered up the papers on his desk, placing them back in the file folder for tomorrow. Just as he put that away, another text came through on his phone. He stiffened...*everywhere.*

The photograph Maisie sent showed her lying on her back, soft lighting all around her. Her hair blanketed the ground behind her. Her dress was pulled down, revealing her gorgeous cleavage.

He texted back: I'll be there in 10.

11

Twinkle lights were strung along the large wooden beams that ran the length of the space that was once a hayloft. It was now Maisie's quiet place. Blankets were laid out in the corner, surrounded by too many pillows to count. As a child, she and Laurel would spend hours up here playing hide-and-seek around the hay bales. Pops hadn't been huge on farming, like his father had, but he had kept a hobby farm for years. Horses for them to ride, goats, sheep, a cow, just furry friends to keep him company, especially after their grandmother passed away.

The space reminded her of simpler times, when things weren't so serious, where everything wasn't on the line.

A sudden creak in the wooden floorboard had her smiling. She took a quick look at her screen. "Eight minutes," she said, looking at Hayes across from her. "Wow, my boobs must have looked great."

Hayes lips curved at the sides. He leaned against the thick wooden pole, arms folded, eyes burning. "Delectable."

"Hmm," she purred, playfully. "I take it since you got here so fast that you're hungry then?"

"Famished." His grin dripped lust.

All day she'd been thinking of him, thinking of *this*. No matter how confusing life got, when they touched, everything was okay. Always. This part was easy. The emotional stuff made everything hard. And she kept thinking, as long as she reminded him how good they were together, showed him how great the future could be, everything would be okay. They would be okay, and they'd figure out the steps to take to find their happiness. A forever kind of happiness. "Oh, that's something we must fix, then." She sat up a little and unzipped the back of her dress, letting the fabric slide off her shoulders. She wasn't wearing a bra. The dress had one built in.

The low groan that spilled from Hayes's mouth made her wet in an instant. The hunger in his wicked gaze as his eyes roamed over her bare breasts was *hot*. He had his T-shirt off a second later, his jeans and boxer briefs dropped next. She wiggled out of her dress and panties as he fetched a condom from his wallet and readied himself.

Before she could make a next move, he was there, placing her down on the pillows, sliding between her legs. The scent of his woodsy cologne wrapped around her as he gathered her in his strong arms, his hard body pressing all the right places. His kiss set her on fire as his tongue sensually stroked hers. A low growl rumbled from his chest, like he could barely get enough of her. Urgency tickled in her belly as his hardened length stroked between her thighs. The need. The desire. She moaned against his mouth, rubbing herself up and down his cock while tangling her fingers into his hair.

God, yes, she wanted this. Wanted him. *Needed* him. She moved faster beneath him, dragging her sex up and down over his rock-hard length. The tease was too much. He was too much. She broke the kiss to rasp, "I need you inside me."

He grunted against her mouth and switched their positions. Now straddling his waist, she stared down at him, feeling herself growing wetter at just the sight of him. My God, Hayes was a dream come true. Strong. Sexy. Pure seduction. She shuddered against the need pulsating through her.

At whatever expression crossed her face, he gave a smile dripping sex, then used both hands to squeeze her bum. "You seem like you know what you're doing. Show me what you've got."

She returned the grin and rocked her hips, sliding up the length of him. "Are you challenging me to see how good I am in bed?"

He moaned, the soft lights showcasing the pleasure washing over his face. "I showed you what I've got, didn't I? Seems only fair."

"Hmmm," she purred, playfully rolling her hips. "I suppose it does."

Challenge accepted, she placed her hands on his chest and shifted her hips slowly until she took the tip of him inside her. Just as slowly, she brought him in deep, all the way to the hilt, letting him feel the gentle squeeze of her. She held his stare, feeling empowered by him watching her so intently. His gaze jerked to her breasts and his moan made goose bumps rise on her arms. He cupped her breasts, and he played there, massaged and squeezed her nipples, awakening every inch of her flesh. Breathless, stretched perfectly by him, she circled her hips, urged on by his needy moans. Beneath her, she took in hard muscles flexing with every stroke. His eyes were dark, hooded. His lips were parted, hers for the taking, and she sealed her mouth over his and began working over him, bringing them higher, slowly.

Until she wanted more.

She rose up and rocked her hips. Harder. Faster.

He groaned at her bouncing breasts, his hands going there to enjoy. "Fucking love looking at you," he growled.

Then those intense whiskey eyes met hers. His guttural groan had her shifting her hips back and forth, the pleasure building. She wanted to get there. She wanted them both to get there. She rode him without inhibition, loud moans ringing out between them, the scent of their musk filling the air.

And there, right when his pleasure peaked, hardening him deep inside her, pinching his expression, she lost sight of everything but her pleasure. She tipped her head back and moved faster. Harder. And when the pleasure rose, she let go, falling into this magical place between them, vaguely aware of Hayes bucking and jerking beneath her, his roar of pleasure drawing out hers.

"You win," he said, sometime later, with a rough laugh.

She chuckled, finding herself tucked into his arms, breathless. Her body tingled from head to toe in pure happiness. "How about we both win? Because we have amazing fucking sex."

He chuckled. "I'm okay with that."

Many, many minutes had passed while they caught their breath and the sweat dried, and they finally recovered from the blissful haze of pleasure, when Hayes said, "I've got some news for you."

"Oh?" she mumbled.

"I went to work for my dad today."

She shot up. His words having the effect of a bucket of ice-cold water being dumped on her. "What?"

His attention fell to her bare breasts before his brow arched. "We should probably get dressed if we're going to have to this conversation."

Her stare fell to his ripped, glistening body, his muscles flexing, and a deep shudder ran through her. "I see your point." She grabbed her panties and dress and slid back into them, while Hayes threw on his jeans and T-shirt. Once she took a seat beside him, the twinkling, lights casting him in a warm glow, she said, "Okay, tell me everything."

"Someone stole your trailer," he said, then gave a small shrug. "I wanted to work the case."

Time slowed around her as she stared into the warm swirls of his eyes. "You went back for...me?"

Something sweet and soft crossed his expression before he pulled her closer, until he lay back on the pillows, tucking her into his side. She stared up at the twinkling lights above them as he ran his fingers through her hair. She swore she could still smell the timothy hay up here, even though it'd been years since they'd had any.

"It's in my nature to fix problems," he explained a moment later. "Sitting on the sidelines wouldn't have worked for me. Last night, I went and saw my father. To work the case, I had to promise six months of my service."

She wasn't even sure what to make of that. He'd just said the other day that going back to the force wasn't on the table. She leaned up enough to get a read on his expression. "Are you sure this is what you want to do?"

Of course, he was locked up tight, his face revealing nothing. "Yes," he said firmly.

Aghast, she blinked at him.

He chuckled softly, tucking her hair behind her ear. "I've surprised you."

"Dumbfounded me is more like it," she muttered. "Just the other day you said being a cop was part of your old life."

"It was, until someone hurt you."

She reeled at that statement. At the meaning in that statement. She slowly shook her head, the ground dropping out from under her. "You're telling me that because someone hurt me, you're now breaking all of your rules and going back to your job on the force?"

He inclined his head. "It's really that simple."

She stared at him as he slid his fingers through her hair, lost in those strong eyes of his. This was anything but simple. Her head spun as she lay back in the crook of his shoulder while his fingers continued to slide over her hair again. "Have you told Nash?"

"I called him on the drive over and explained the situation."

"Is he upset?"

"Of course not. He's got access to a few good guys that can fill my place easily enough." His voice softened. "But I enjoy working for him, so on my days off, I'll put in a few hours at the farm."

"It won't be too much for you?"

"Nah. It's either spend that time at the farm or the gym."

"True."

"Besides, it's not like once my six months of service are up, I can't go back to the farm full-time."

She knew the answer to her next question but wondered if Hayes did. She sank into the heat of his hold, and asked, "Why do you think your dad asked for six months of your service?"

"He thinks I'll remember how much I love being a cop and decide to stay."

She blew out a quick breath, relieved he knew it too. His

father's insistence to get Hayes back on the force didn't surprise her. *Everyone* knew that's where Hayes belonged, but what confused Maisie was why, if he'd been so adamant to stay away from the force, he'd gone back. For her. "Today you worked my case, then?"

His deep voice filled the empty space. "Unofficially at the moment, until all the documents go through. The perks of working in a small town, where the chief of police is your father."

She lifted her head again, gazed into the softness of his eyes. "It's incredibly sweet that you're doing this for me. I'm not sure what to say."

He brushed his knuckles against her cheek and smiled tenderly. "You've been there for me in times when anyone else would have turned away. You don't need to say a damn thing."

She leaned into his touch, aware of a truth she never really saw until he'd rejoined the force. Probably also because of her conversation with Luna this morning about Hayes keeping a secret. Before now, Maisie never questioned his motives, thinking it all had to do with Laurel. She thought he couldn't be a cop anymore because he'd lost his wife in a violent crime. That he couldn't care deeply again, because his wife had died. That no one else mattered beyond his own pain. But his actions blew those theories apart.

Her world spun away from her. "Are you keeping something from me?"

He went still. "Like what?"

She sat up again to watch his expression. "I went to see Luna Whittle this morning—"

His brows shot up. "The psychic in town?"

"Yup, her." Maisie hesitated then forced the words from

her dry throat. "She told me that you're keeping a secret from me."

His expression did the cop thing. It went blank, hard. "You're actually listening to a psychic?"

She nodded without shame. "I'm getting all the help I can right now. And don't dodge the question. Are you?"

He watched her for a long moment. His lips parted like he was about to admit a truth that, by tightness of his jaw, was difficult. But then he shook his head, tucking her hair behind her ear. "Your psychic is wrong. I'm not hiding anything."

Maisie's internal alarms sounded. She wasn't sure if she should be thrilled to know that Luna was correct, or annoyed that Hayes was keeping something from her. "Really? Nothing to tell me?"

His gaze averted to the twinkling lights above them. "No, nothing."

In that hollow tone of his voice, clarity hit Maisie. That *nothing,* whatever it may be, was the very thing keeping them from having *everything.*

12

The next morning, Maisie sat on her narrow bed, the same bed she'd had for more years than she dared count. Her bedroom consisted of a desk, a chest of drawers, a mirror, a chair, and a nightstand. She'd matched it with soft lilac bedsheets and a white duvet. Her room caught the morning sun, and she looked over at her dresser, finding her tote bag. Her heart reached for her paintbrushes and canvas, but the splint on her finger remained, even if the pain had diminished, and drawing anything polished was definitely not in the plans. It felt like forever since she'd created anything. She hopped out of bed to grab her sketch book, which was about the only thing she could do with a broken finger, when her grandfather's letter fell out onto the floor. She froze midstep and then laughed softly at herself. Luna had her thinking Pops was following her all over the place. She grabbed the letter from the floor and then returned to her bed.

Beams of sunlight shone on her duvet as she took out her sketch pad and pencil. She opened the letter and read the quote again: *The greatest danger for most of us is not that our aim is too high and we miss it, but that it is too low and we reach it.*

She never really understood that quote before, but for some reason it resonated now. Maybe because of what Clara said the other night about the broken mug. *"He told you no one was like you. That most people would have thrown it out. But you looked at something broken and made it beautiful. That was your gift to the world."*

Every day since the brewery opened, Maisie had been trying to fit into Clara's box and do things her sister's way. She'd failed miserably. Over and over again. With Luna's advice humming in her ear, Maisie wondered what would happen if she did something her way, in her style. And that, instead of setting her aim so low that her only wish was to survive the festivals and fulfill Pops's final wish, maybe she needed to set the bar higher. To do things in a way that was true to herself. To figure out what the brewery needed from her. And a little bit of beauty never hurt anyone.

An idea suddenly came to her, as if Pops were whispering the words into her ear. She grabbed her cell and texted her sisters and Penelope: `Family meeting in 20.` The dings of her phone indicated they'd responded. Maisie didn't let the notifications distract her, she began awkwardly sketching with the splint in the way, her hand flowing fast over the page, her imagination coming to life before her eyes.

When she finally stopped, she looked down at the shadowed drawing. It definitely wasn't a masterpiece, but it showed her intent. "Yeah, yeah, Pops. I get it now," she said to herself. This whole time, she'd been following Clara and Amelia. But she needed to lead. With a smile, she hopped up and hurried to get dressed and threw her hair up in a messy bun.

Right on time, she trotted down the staircase, finding her sisters and Penelope sitting at the kitchen table, a box of Danishes in the center. Maisie ignored those and slapped the drawing down on the page.

Clara studied the piece of paper. "Not your usual beauty. What exactly am I looking at here?"

"Our barn."

"Okay," Clara said slowly then looked to Maisie with lifted brows. "You want to decorate it?"

The drawing depicted her favorite spot, where she'd been with Hayes. Romantic and whimsical, she'd drawn that same décor throughout the entire brewery. "We needed that last festival to make us stand out. We all know that. It's going to hurt us and hurt big time. We needed that final push for our social media. That didn't happen. But who's to say we can't bring the party here?"

Amelia took the piece of paper. "To the barn?"

"Yes," Maisie said. "We put on a festival of our own, but make it even better. Our type of party, done our way."

Clara gazed at her with intense focus. "Go on."

Maisie drew in a big, deep breath, her belly filled with butterflies, and sat next to Penelope. "Okay, we share the party all over social media. We've got the beer, and this is our chance. We take what we've got that's not already promised to the restaurants and bars here, and we serve it until it runs out. We all know this is our only shot. We either bring out the big guns or go home. We can bring in a band, set up a dance floor outside the barn or something."

Penelope asked, "But where would you get a band on such short notice?"

Maisie didn't even hesitate, already thinking all this through. "First, let's aim to have the party in a week. That'll give us the time we need to get the event out there. Second, I thought we could approach Megan." She was Nash's wife and owned the best bar in town, Kinky Spurs. They had an in-house band, and Maisie was pretty sure she'd agree to help out.

Silence drifted around the table. All eyes on Clara. She finally exhaled deeply and looked to Maisie with a smile. "This idea didn't come from Luna Whittle, right?"

Maisie snorted a laugh. "No, of course not." Well, yeah, it kind of did, but Clara in her non-believing ways didn't have to know that. "Please. Put me out of my misery. What do you think?"

"I think"—Clara scanned the drawing again—"I think your idea is beautiful, and I can't wait to see it in real life."

Amelia and Penelope squealed.

"Really?" Maisie asked, bolting from the chair. "After all that's happened, you're actually going to let me do this?"

Clara nodded and rose. "I never said we couldn't do things your way; you just never offered any ideas." She gave Maisie a warm hug. "Make it happen. Let me know the date."

When she left the room, Maisie exchanged a long look with Penelope and Amelia. "Did that just happen?" she asked softly.

Amelia nodded and kissed Maisie on the cheek. "You done good, Maisie-Moo. Let me know if you need any help on my end." And then she was gone too.

"Pinch me," Maisie said to Penelope. "Let me know I'm not dreaming."

Penelope pinched Maisie's arm. Hard.

"Ow," Maisie gasped.

"Nope, not dreaming," Penelope said with a sly smile, picking up her half-finished Danish off the table. "Want me to come to Kinky Spurs with you?"

Maisie considered. Maybe for the first time ever in her life, she said, "I actually think I need to do this myself."

A half an hour later, she was doing exactly that, walking into Kinky Spurs alone. The bar on Main Street had wood paneling from floor to ceiling, with the space basically being a large rectangle bookended by two stages. One stage had the band's instruments, the other had a mechanical bull with mats surrounding it. Reclaimed wood tables were spread out between the two stages, and the place smelled like peanuts and beer.

Behind the bar was Megan Blackshaw. She was trim, with freckles dusting her nose, wavy sandy-brown hair, and she had one crystal blue eye and the other was a warm brown. Behind her was a bright pink neon KINKY SPURS sign with large deer antlers overtop. At this time of day, it was rare there was a customer, but Maisie often did beer deliveries in the morning.

"Hi, Megan," Maisie said, shutting the front door behind her.

Megan lifted her head from her paperwork and greeted Maisie with a kind smile. "Hey. I wasn't expecting any deliveries today."

"That's actually not why I'm here," Maisie explained, reaching the bar and sliding onto one of the metal stools. "I have a favor to ask."

Megan placed her pen down, giving Maisie her full attention. "Hit me with it."

"Okay, so I guess I'll start at the beginning..." Maisie relayed every little thing that happened from the beginning of the festival to now, to how much they still needed to create buzz about the brewery. "Without this final festival, we risk another brewery standing out and having a better chance at getting a distributor."

"And you can't have that," Megan agreed with a nod. "What can I do to help?"

"I wondered if I could rent your band?"

"For a party?"

Maisie nodded. "I've decided to throw a big barn dance at the brewery. I admit I'm not exactly sure how to do all that, but I figured getting a band is a good first step."

Something sweet and infectious crossed Megan's face as she tilted her head. "You know, today must be your lucky day. I happen to know how to throw a good party."

She most certainly did. Megan wasn't even thirty years old and she'd made her bar a huge success. Nothing in town could compete with it and no one even tried. "Is that an offer to help me with this?" Maisie asked gently.

"Of course!" Megan said. "Us boss girls in River Rock need to stick together. Not only am I sure the band will play for you, but I've got all morning to help you brainstorm the hell of out of this party."

Luna's words flowed through Maisie's mind: *Ask for help. It's out there.* Maisie managed, "Thank you."

"You don't need to thank me," Megan said, smiling warmly. "Your Pops came into my bar when I first opened. He stopped in every day for a beer, and we'd talk for hours. Whatever I can do for him, and you and your sisters, I'll do without question." Megan strode around the bar and sat beside Maisie on the stool. "What do you have so far?"

Maisie took the piece of paper from her pocket. For the first time, she didn't feel foolish for not having a business plan like Clara would. She handed Megan her drawing. "I've got the décor."

"Wow," Megan said, awe in her voice. "Maybe you could make this a monthly thing at the brewery. Or even host wedding receptions and things like that." Her gaze met Maisie's. "This is really beautiful, Maisie. Truly."

Maisie's heart swelled a hundred sizes bigger. "Thanks." And for the first time, she felt like she was finally getting something right.

<hr>

Hayes pushed away the documents on his desk and cursed. The case was going nowhere, and the day had already been long, even though it was only midafternoon. He'd continued to watch the surveillance videos from every angle the amusement park offered up, but he'd hit dead end after dead end. Hayes doubted the theft was by chance. Even though he spotted the guy who broke into his truck, dressed in a dark hoody, the thief clearly knew where the security cameras were and avoided being recognized. He also hadn't slowly walked up the truck. He strode toward it with purpose, and had gotten inside fast, signifying to Hayes he already knew the truck and trailer were there. That he'd already scoped it out, meaning he had to have already been at the amusement park. Hayes stayed on this footage, watching every single person who came to the amusement park, feeling like the clue he needed to find another way to identify the criminal was right there. Hayes studied the lanky guy's mannerisms. He had a subtle limp in his right leg. While Detective Stewart had seen this video too, Hayes still felt compelled to stay there to watch.

On top of that, thoughts of Maisie kept distracting him. He felt edgy, restless...uncomfortable. For a long time, she'd made all that go away. Determined to take the break he needed, and after a quick call to Nash's brother, Shep Black-

shaw, Hayes texted Maisie: Can you meet me at
Blackshaw Cattle Guest Ranch?

What time?

An hour.

See ya there.

Wear jeans.

This sounds very PG rated.

Hayes chuckled. Will you be disappointed if
it is?

I'll let you know when I get there. See
you soonish.

Hayes heaved a long sigh down at the papers strewn out
on his desk. The answer was right there in front of him. He
could nearly taste it. Frustrated, he checked his email once
more, but Neil hadn't sent anything along to indicate he was
any further ahead in the investigation. The bigger problem?
Time was running out. His father was being lenient by
letting Hayes work this case. If nothing developed soon, the
case would be considered cold and shoved aside. Hayes
couldn't allow that to happen. He needed this solved. For
Maisie.

He left the station and drove the twenty minutes to the
cattle ranch. When he arrived at the big gates, he headed
past the wrought iron sign that read: BLACKSHAW
CATTLE CO. AND GUEST RANCH. For years, the Blackshaw family had owned the largest cattle ranch in Colorado,
but when their company faced hardship after Nash's father
died, they'd turned business into a working dude ranch.
They'd found success there.

Hayes worked his way up the long driveway with mature
evergreen trees hugging the lane. The narrow path soon
opened to the guest ranch. Straight ahead was a stone farmhouse, where Nash grew up with his older brothers. On the

right were twelve log cabins where the guests from the dude ranch stayed. In the middle was a large limestone fire pit and Adirondack chairs.

As he slowed his rental truck, he spotted Shep, Nash's older brother, exiting the barn with two tacked up horses at his side. His eyes were a silvery blue, his hair dark brown, and there was nothing fancy about him. He was a home-grown country man, with a dark-brown cowboy hat, plaid button-down, worn blue jeans, and scuffed brown boots. Hayes quickly parked and got out of his truck. "Can't tell you how much I appreciate this," Hayes said by way of greeting. He needed a ride. The freedom. The quiet. And the dude ranch had well-trained horses.

Shep gave an easy smile. "It's not a problem. These two could use a good ride out anyway." He offered Hayes the reins. "Tie 'em back up at the corral when you're done. Some of the boys are out on a ride with our newest guests. They'll put them away when they get back."

"Will do."

Shep looked like he was fighting a smile. "Try not to fall off these ones."

"Ha," Hayes said with a snort. "These ones are sane. Unlike the horses at your brother's place."

"Yeah, but you are the one that rides them," Shep shot over his shoulder as he walked away.

Hayes shook his head and chuckled.

The crunch of gravel sounded behind him. Hayes turned to find Maisie's MINI coming up the driveway. The heavy weight on his chest slowly lessened.

After she parked next to his truck, she jumped out of her car. "Ah-ha, I knew it. We're going for a ride, aren't we?"

Hayes noted her cowboy boots and her tan cowboy hat sitting atop her wavy hair. She wore a flowered blouse and tight jeans that made focusing on anything but her killer body difficult. He cleared his throat and nodded. "I needed a break from the case and thought you could use one too."

She smiled when she reached him. "A break is good." Boldly, she rose on her tiptoes and kissed him like it was the most natural thing she'd ever done.

Up until this moment, he never realized how much he liked that about Maisie. Everything with Maisie was easy. Like a breath of fresh air. Her soft lips brushed sweetly and perfectly against his, making him want to deepen the kiss until they were both breathless and sweaty. He forced himself to back away. He hadn't invited her here for that, no matter what his body wanted. He gestured at the smaller horse. "Up you go." She sidled up to the horse, took hold of the reins, and grabbed the horn of the saddle. He took her knee, and she bounced once on her foot before he hoisted her up. He adjusted the stirrups to her size. "How long has it been since you've ridden?"

"Years, but I'm pretty sure I'll be okay." She winked at him. "As long as you can catch me." She spun the horse, gave the mare a kick and cantered off toward the hill at the back of the house that led to the vast Colorado meadows.

Hayes laughed, shoved his foot in the stirrup, which was close enough to his height to be comfortable and he clicked his tongue. The chestnut horse cantered off easily, and once Hayes passed the house, he gave the horse a slight squeezing and opened him up to a gallop. The scent of warm earth carried along the breeze, the sun set over the snowy, peaked mountains, and the grasses blew in the wind as Hayes rushed by.

When he caught up to Maisie, she laughed, slowing the mare to a walk. "Dammit, I should have gone faster."

He arched an eyebrow at her. "Trying to show me up, huh?"

"Always." Her eyes warmed under the beams of sunlight before she turned to glance out in front of her.

Hayes followed her gaze, discovering the reason. Deer grazed off in the distance. Shadows drifted over the meadow as clouds passed overhead. The air always smelled cleaner out here. Fresher. Comfortable silence fell between them as Hayes led them through a trail cut out in the thick forest and then up another small hill. They moved closer to the mountains until they reached the stream bubbling across the meadow. "Let's hang here for a bit," he said.

She turned to him with a smile. "Love to."

He dismounted, as she did, and then he tied their horses to a tree, letting them graze on the long grasses.

"I've got some news today," she said, taking off her boots and socks, and rolling up her jeans. She stuck her feet in the stream. "Good news for change."

"Oh?" He sat in next to her on mossy rocks. "Do tell."

She gave him a cute smile. "In a week, I'm holding a big barn dance at the brewery, since we couldn't get to the festival. Megan's going to help with the band and giving me some pointers about it all."

His chest expanded at the pride in her face. "This was your idea?"

She gave a firm nod. "Clara even went for it. Can you believe it?"

"Yes, I can believe it," he told her. "Your ideas are amazing, Maisie." Everything about her was amazing. He liked the cute smile she gave and he reached for a pebble next to him. He sent it skipping down the stream. "Is everyone welcome?"

"If you mean you, then yes, you're welcome. Always."

The softness in her voice drew his gaze. "Spread the word as much as you can. I know everyone here in River Rock will be in for this party, but we need to reach people outside of the locals."

He nodded. "What's your plan so far?"

"Tomorrow I'm putting posters up in all the bars that Megan and I can think of. Social media will hopefully help us a ton. Then it's just word of mouth, connecting with the right people to make it happen."

"Sounds like you got it all figured out."

She smiled softly. "You know, I think I actually do, which is weird. I'm usually running around with no idea what I'm doing, but this...it actually feels really good." He returned the smile, but that smile faded quick, when something changed in her expression. She stared at him openly, with emotion. "I guess that brings me to something I've been putting off."

He glanced back at her, the sun catching the warmer tones in her eyes. "Which is?"

"Us. Talking about what we're doing here."

His chest tightened and he glanced back at the stream. "Is it necessary to talk about anything?" He glanced sidelong at her. "We're good, aren't we?"

"Good, yes, but..." Her eyes searched his. "But after I went to see Luna, I guess everything she said to me got me thinking about some tough questions."

"You should speak up," he said, even though he knew this would backfire on him.

She watched him a long moment and then cringed a little. "Do you think you could ever love me? Like, see a future with me? Is that, after all we've been through, even possible?"

Her ability to be a straight shooter always amazed him.

That's partly what pulled him out of the darkness, because she saw a way out of it, and he followed her past his grief. But what she asked...the answer felt so fucking difficult to give her. He ran a hand over his face, so close to opening his mouth and just laying it all out there. But he thought it was kinder to hold back, because he still didn't know how he was going to tell her about Laurel. "I don't want to promise you something I don't know I can give you. This is...I don't want to mess this up with us. I definitely don't want to hurt you."

She gave him a look that pierced right through him. "Hayes, you're not the only one dealing with this. Do you think this isn't weird for me too? Laurel was my best friend. We grew up together. You two were supposed to grow old together. But Laurel's gone, and there's all this"—she waved between them—"stuff going on."

Hayes couldn't take his eyes off her, this woman who changed everything for him, as she added, "I've thought about this, believe me. A thousand times. I felt guilty, hated myself, and then felt guilty all over again for having feelings for you. But I always came back to the same conclusion, Laurel wouldn't hate me for anything I felt. That's not how our love worked. And I know for certain that Laurel wouldn't want you to ignore that we're happy, no matter what's going in that head of yours. She wouldn't want you to hold back. You know that."

He slowly nodded, well aware. "I do know that."

"Then what's the problem? Why do I feel like you're a step behind me?" she asked, leveling him with that potent stare. "Tell me. We'll work through it."

His lips parted to admit all his weaknesses and his fears. That he'd failed to protect his wife and love her like she deserved. That he'd ruined Maisie's life because of it. But nothing came out. What would happen if he told her the truth about Laurel's death? If he broke her heart all over again? Would she look at him differently? He wondered how he would survive if she walked away. Emotion crept up his throat, the air nearly impossible to inhale. He shut his eyes, feeling like a damn coward when all she'd shown was strength. When he looked at her again, her chin quivered, tears welling in her eyes.

"Okay, so you're not ready yet," she said softly and rose.

He stood with her. "Wait."

She moved to the horses and untied them. "Let's just ride and not talk. I'm okay with that."

He strode toward her, the world feeling like it was rushing by. All the things he wanted to stay stuck deep in his throat. All the fears roaring through his mind. She'd pulled him out of his darkest times, he owed her everything. And yet, she never demanded a damn thing.

He helped her mount her horse and then hopped on his. She turned to him with one of her tender smiles, understanding he needed more time. Always understanding exactly what he needed. "Ready?"

But this time, he saw something different. Something that turned his blood ice cold. She faked that smile. For *him*. To be there for him. To support him through his pain. To be his friend. To give him every fucking thing he needed. She put her heart out there, when she knew he could very well crush it. "Yeah, lead the way," he barely managed.

She turned her horse away and led like she had for a long time, pulling him out of the shadows surrounding his life. She'd done that for so long.

And it suddenly felt wrong.

13

_____

One week later, Maisie covered a yawn with her hand. She was sure she had never worked as hard in her life as she had these past seven days, but all those hours of planning had finally paid off. Everyone helped, including her sisters, Megan, Penelope, and Hayes. He handled all the heavy lifting since her broken finger still got in the way. She and Hayes hadn't talked about _them_ since the day at the creek, and between getting ready for the big bash, and Hayes still working her case, she'd barely seen him, except when he stopped in with food or to help lift the stuff too heavy for Clara and Amelia. But those little things, supporting her during this event, meant everything. It was clear he wasn't where she was yet, and she couldn't blame him for that.

Besides that hiccup, the world, for once, was being kind and gave her a beautiful night for the barn dance. The sky was clear, without a cloud in sight, a blanket of twinkling stars sparkling through the darkness. String lights hung from the big wooden beams throughout the barn across to the steel kegs, igniting a soft glow that spilled out onto the dance floor just outside the barn. Maisie filled the inside of the barn with flowers and plants, making the space warm and inviting. They had rented a small stage and a wooden dance floor from a place in Colorado Springs, and the Kinky Spurs band played for the crowd. Penelope, along with a couple of Kinky Spurs waitresses, worked at the makeshift bar they'd set up in the parking lot. They tended to the crowd that had come from all over Colorado for the free beer and the fun night of some good ol' country music.

"Amazing turnout," Clara said with a smile, sidling up to Maisie. She had a beer in her hand, her tight jeans on, and an even tighter black tank top. Her fiery red hair was straightened, her makeup a little darker. Mason was staying at the sitter's tonight.

Maisie smiled, warmth radiating through her chest at the pride in Clara's voice. "I really hope it's enough to make us stand out."

Clara scanned the crowd of partygoers. Her bright eyes met Maisie. "I'd say you've pulled off the impossible, Maisie. Look at what you did here. I never would have even dreamed of making this happen."

Maisie snorted and gently pointed out. "Well, that's 'cause you would have made it to the festival."

"True." Clara nudged Maisie's shoulder. "But maybe it's good you didn't. Maybe you had to fail there to make this happen here."

"Let's hope so," Maisie agreed, praying that was true. There was absolutely no way of telling if this party would simply be a party that the townsfolk talked about, or if it would gain some traction through social media. But one thing Masie knew for certain, she'd made a plan and executed it. Considering all she'd been doing lately was failing, this felt good.

The crowd gave off thunderous applause as the band finished a song, the lights flashing blue and red and green into the dark night. The lead singer picked right up again with his gravelly voice.

"Is Hayes coming tonight?"

Maisie shrugged at Clara. "I thought he'd be here already." She couldn't help wondering if pushing him too fast had made him shut down, and in turn, shut her out. There were no hot nights. No incredible rides through the meadows. He'd come to the brewery, supported her, but left quickly. "I'm sure he'll be here soon." She hoped.

Clara nodded, and then her gaze landed on something over Maisie's shoulder.

"Trouble," she said with a frown.

Maisie glanced over her shoulder. Immediately, her heart broke at the sight of Amelia and her fiancé, Luka, in a heated argument. Luka had a good couple of inches on Amelia, his lips a bit pouty, his jaw square, his hair dark and styled. All together, it made Luka very handsome, but he had barely been to the brewery lately. Amelia met Luka in college. They became engaged before she left Denver. Now, even Maisie saw they were struggling to adjust to their new life with Amelia living in River Rock and Luka living in Denver. Luka was a big city guy, working in finance. He didn't belong in River Rock, but Amelia did. "What's that all about?" Maisie asked Clara.

"He's probably being an asshole like always," her sister muttered.

Luka didn't deserve Amelia. Everyone knew it, only Amelia couldn't see past her love to realize it. Maisie was absolutely certain that one day, Luka was going to break Amelia's heart.

The yelling match finally stopped and Amelia's gaze

connected with Maisie. "Shit!" Maisie gasped, looking everywhere but behind her. "Look busy. She's coming this way."

Clara stared straight ahead, a pillar of strength.

"I know you two were watching us," Amelia said, sidling up next to Clara.

Maisie turned, her heart squeezing at Amelia's tears. "Are you okay?"

"Not really." Amelia wiped a tear.

Clara glared at Luka's back as he walked away. "What did the dipshit do this time?"

"I've told you to stop calling him that," Amelia snapped, offering a glare that should have burned off Clara's eyebrows. "He just can't stay tonight, that's all."

"Oh yeah," Clara countered. "He's got somewhere better to be?"

Amelia's cheeks filled with color. She looked down at her boots. "There's a game tonight. He's got money on it."

"Sounds very important," Clara muttered. She gave a heavy sigh, and said to Maisie, "Let's stay focused. Nothing personal affects tonight. All right?"

"Of course," Maisie said, taking Amelia's shaky hand.

"Why are you crying?"

Beckett's hard voice snapped Maisie's head to him. He looked like he was counting every one of Amelia's tears to make someone pay for those tears later.

"I'm fine," Amelia said after a few tense seconds, swiping at the tears on her face. "I'm just emotional. It's been a stressful week."

Beckett frowned, obviously not believing her.

Even Maisie didn't believe Amelia. She wanted to shake Amelia by the shoulders and scream, *You belong with Beckett. Dump Luka's ass. Wake up!* But Amelia didn't hear much of anything lately, not when it came to her heart.

"You're right," Maisie finally agreed, lacing her arm with Amelia's. "It has been a stressful week."

Beckett's gaze fell over to where Clara had been looking, obviously at Luka. The look he gave him promised death. But his eyes gentled when they landed back on Amelia. "Come on, let's go get a beer. I'm sure you've saved a dance for me."

Amelia nodded and laughed softly through the tears. "That sounds much better than standing here crying about nothing."

Maisie watched them walk off toward Penelope and the other bartenders serving up Foxy Diva. Beckett kept his hands in his pockets. He did that a lot around her. Maisie was sure the move had become a habit, so he didn't accidentally touch her. He'd been such a good friend to Amelia, no matter what happened between them. Maisie hoped they could find their way back to each other.

"Maisie."

She whirled around at the familiar voice, her stomach somersaulting a little as she gazed into the sparkling blue eyes that had once won her over. Only, Seth had grown up in the few years it'd been since she'd seen him last. Gone was his baby face. In place, was a sculpted man, filled out with a toned body. "Seth, hi."

He gave a crooked smile. "Hey."

"I thought you moved to Boulder?" Or at least that's the last thing she'd heard.

"Yeah, I did." He gestured out at the party. "Got word of this. Wanted to come see it for myself."

"Well, thanks for coming," Maisie said, still reeling. She never expected to see Seth again. She quickly gestured at Clara next to her. "You remember my sister, Clara."

"Yeah," Seth said. "Hey."

Clara gave him a quick smile. "Good to see you again." To Maisie, she added, "I've got the night off and I'm determined to have some fun." She lifted her beer. "But I need more of these before I'll get out on that dance floor. Come find me if you need me."

"I'm fine," Maisie said, giving her a little shove toward Penelope. "Enjoy yourself."

When Clara faded into the crowd, Seth said, "You look really good."

Maisie turned back to Seth with a smile. "You too. You've gotten so...*strong.*"

His mouth twitched. "I work for the Boulder fire department now. I have some good training buddies there." Those captivating eyes scanned over the crowd again. "I've got to admit, I wasn't expecting you to end up at a brewery. What happened to your art?"

The question tugged at her heart. She felt like a totally different person than when she knew Seth. She had dreams of owning an art studio, selling her work, teaching others how to draw. Setting her own schedule. Making the rules. She never realized how much those dreams slipped away until she stared into Seth's familiar eyes. She shrugged. "Life happened." That was the simple answer.

"Ah," he agreed with an understanding nod. "Life can do that."

She watched him a minute, seeing why she liked Seth so much back in the day. He was hot, uncomplicated. But more importantly, she almost wished she could go back to that person she was when she with him. Laurel's best friend, the free spirit, with all her dreams ahead of her.

She didn't even know that person anymore. She was sleeping with Laurel's husband. Her dreams of an art studio were gone. Her soul not as free as it once had been. More guarded, it occurred to her now.

Seth caught her watching him and gave her a sexy smile, gesturing at the dance floor and offering his hand. "Want to get out there? For old times' sake."

"Why not." She smiled, sliding her hand into his familiar touch, reminded, if only for this moment, of the person she'd left behind.

A week had gone by since Maisie's case had grown cold, and that time had ticked by slowly. Hayes's father had Hayes drive along with a rookie on his first few days out as a new beat cop, but Hayes would return to the surveillance footage in his spare time. Frustratingly, nothing in the footage from the day he and Maisie had been at the amusement park showed more on his suspect. From what he'd learned through the investigation, there had been three other car thefts at the park. While Hayes knew the suspect was the same by that subtle limp in the footage, he couldn't identify the prick, so he had no way to find and arrest him. He tried to follow the stolen cars through tolls and other security footage, but had no luck. He ate his dinner at his desk, stuck on finding the clue that would break the case wide open. He rolled his shoulders for the millionth time today, nearly crawling out of his skin for reasons that had nothing to do with this case. He should be at the brewery now. Maisie, no doubt, awaited him, but his head had been fucking with him all day. What she'd said to him a week ago at the creek slammed against his heart. She deserved answers to the questions she'd asked. Why the fuck couldn't he give them to her?

His heart rate kicked up and he rubbed his face, reminding himself of what was important. First, find the bastard who burned her trailer. Then, deal with the rest.

The timestamp on the video he was currently watching was dated a week before they visited the amusement park, and not around any of the times the other cars were stolen. He was grasping at straws. Hayes reached for his coffee that was cool now and took a sip when his cell rang next to his keyboard. Warmth touched him when he saw the screen.

"Hi, Mom," he said by way of greeting.

"Hi, honey, how are things?"

Mom's voice held a sweet edge, beyond nurturing. Likely part of what made her an incredible nurse. "Good and interesting, I would say."

His mother laughed softly. "I suppose that's very much true, since I've heard you decided to go back to work with your father."

Hayes restrained the roll of his eyes, glancing at his father's office instead. Dad wasn't in tonight, having called it a day a few hours ago. It came as no surprise to Hayes his mother had found out about him accepting the position with his father. Hayes's parents texted each other. Before texting was a thing, they exchanged phone calls. He respected the hell out of them for that, the way they put their shit aside to be good co-parents. Though at thirty-one, he found their conversations near laughable. "Dad told you?"

A pause. "He just gave me the heads-up."

In case Hayes needed more emotional support was what she left out. "No need for a heads-up. Everything's fine."

"Is it? Truly?"

"Yes." He ran a hand through his hair, wishing he'd have left earlier to head home for a shower before going to see Maisie tonight. He felt like crawling out of his skin, and even then, he might not even feel clean. "I'm taking this one step at time. First step is finding out who stole Maisie's trailer."

"It's just terrible," his mother said. "That poor woman. She's so sweet and kind, doesn't need this kind of stress."

"You're right, she doesn't."

Mom paused again. This time, her voice lifted slightly. "Your father may have mentioned he thought something was going on between you and Maisie."

Hayes rubbed at his sore neck muscles, wishing now his parents didn't share so much about his life. "Did he?"

"Mm-hmm," Mom said. And waited.

Hayes blew out a breath, shaking his head. "We're... she's...."

The silence on the end of the phone was deafening before Mom burst out laughing. "Hayes Taylor, I really hope you are clearer with Maisie than that."

Tension tightened his chest until breathing became difficult. "This is all new. We're taking it slow." A bullshit answer.

Mom hesitated a little longer, as if she read right through him. "Well, whatever is going on, I think it's really great, regardless if there are some...kinks to be worked out. Maisie's such a darling. You two have been through a lot together. It's about time you both had some happiness in your lives."

It should be that simple. But life wasn't fucking simple.

The room began swallowing him up, the walls closing in tighter and tighter. And yet, the unknown left him feeling like he was drowning with no way to get in air. He wanted to offer Maisie everything. All the things she deserved, and even more than that. But he couldn't fathom seeing pain in her eyes—pain he caused. And yet, *and yet,* there was no way forward without admitting how he failed to protect Laurel. That he was the very reason she was dead. That his kindness to a criminal had gotten her best friend killed. He'd done that. Just him. "Listen, Mom, I've got to run," he said, shutting his eyes to keep the room from spinning.

Mom's voice softened. "Okay. I miss you and love you, and hope you come out to see me soon."

"You know I will. Love you too." He hung up the phone as fast as he could, his heartbeat thundering in his ears. He breathed deep. Once. Twice. Again. And again. In through his nose, out his mouth. Until the panic gripping him eased, and he focused on his surroundings. On the voices around him. The electronic doors opening and closing. The sirens sounding from outside.

When he felt cemented back in his body, he reopened his eyes and reminded himself of his plan. First, catch the bastard. Then, deal with the rest.

He clicked the video again and began watching cars pulling into the parking lot and leaving. He didn't pay any attention to the families coming and going, but focused on the singles. He took another sip of his cold coffee when he caught a tall, lanky man exiting a black car, the same man he'd seen steal Maisie's trailer and the other cars too.

First, Hayes noticed the car was a Toyota Prius. Then he zoomed in on the man, who didn't move toward the park's entrance but studied the cars around him. More importantly, this man had a slight limp.

Better yet, Hayes had a license plate number.

The phone was in his hand in an instant. When Neil answered, Hayes said, "I've got a suspect."

That high Hayes felt when he'd said those four words

lasted for the next hour until Hayes arrived at the brewery and that high plummeted.

Not at the apparent success that Maisie's homegrown beer festival had become, but at her on the dance floor, her hands in the air, a beaming smile on her face. That gorgeous smile wasn't aimed at Hayes. It was aimed at her ex-boyfriend, Seth, the prick that Hayes had sworn he'd make pay for bailing on Maisie like he did.

Only now, Hayes couldn't move, couldn't breathe.

"Better that you see it now than later."

At Clara's sharp voice, he glanced next to him, finding the eldest Carter sister, staring out at Maisie.

She finally looked Hayes's way and gave a knowing look. "She's given you two years. You've got her heart, whether you want to admit that or not. She deserves more than a friend with benefits."

He forced the words out from deep in his dry throat. "I know that."

"Do you?" Clara asked, eyes wide with clear surprise. "Because I would think out of anyone, you would understand how short life can be."

He swallowed back the emotion. "I do." Fuck, did he ever.

The band hammered out the country song, the crowd singing along to the music. Clara studied Maisie, her head tilting, her expression soft. "It's a beautiful thing, isn't it? No matter how much pain and darkness has touched her life, she's always there, just like that, bringing smiles to everyone around her. An angel right here on earth for all of us who need it."

Hayes had never heard her explained that way, but that's exactly what Maisie was. His guardian angel, guiding him these last years.

Clara placed her hand on Hayes's arm, the contact felt oddly warm. "Imagine a world where Maisie was given that love back."

The power of her statement was a direct hit to Hayes's gut. Only his pride kept him from dropping to his knees and gasping for breath.

Clara stared right through him, a loving sister who wasn't about to back down, but she offered him a kind smile. "Thanks for all you did to help her these past two weeks. I won't forget that anytime soon."

And with the ground shaking beneath him, his heartbeat roaring in his ears, she walked away.

Almost as if she sensed his emotion and his need of her like she always did, Maisie spun around, her eyes connecting with his. Her smile brightened. She said something to Seth and then bounced her way over. Then, like she always did, she threw her arms around him like he deserved it. "You're finally here."

But he didn't deserve her. He forced himself to let go. "I can't stay I'm afraid." Yeah, he could, but now he knew, he shouldn't.

"Oh no," she said, pulverizing him with those sweet eyes. "Why?"

"I found our suspect."

She slapped his arm, eyes huge and twinkling. "You did not?"

He nodded, desperate to pull her close again. He shoved his hands into his pockets, clenching his fists tight. "Detective Stewart is adding me onto the conference call, but I wanted to come by and see what you've done here." He took in the crowd on the dance floor and the crowd at the bar before he forced a smile. "It's absolutely beautiful...and busy."

"Right?" She gave a shit-eating grin, totally lit up, and bounced on the balls of her feet. "I still can't believe it all worked out, but enough about me." Then her stare turned deeper, searching. "What's wrong?"

"Nothing," he said immediately. "Just tired." Lies. All fucking lies. "Enjoy tonight. You deserve every minute of this." He pulled his hands out of his pockets and gathered her in his arms, inhaled her coconut-scented shampoo, and kissed the top of her head. "I'll call tomorrow."

"Okay," she said tightly, leaning away, her eyes searching his again. "You sure everything is okay?"

This time, he only nodded.

The squinting of her eyes told him she read right through him. "Hayes—"

The world began swallowing him up again, because Clara was right. Maisie, in all her beauty and kind heart, deserved more. "Enjoy tonight, Maisie."

14

Late the next afternoon, Maisie stretched out her legs, placing her ankles up on the armrest between Clara and Amelia in the back seat of Clara's sedan and sighed in happiness. Everything hurt, most of all her broken finger. She'd obviously overdone it last night, and not even the painkillers touched the pain today. It didn't help that she and her sisters, along with Penelope, spent the day cleaning up their property after last night's bash and took down the stage and dance floor. By the end of their cleaning, if Maisie never saw another plastic cup, she'd consider that a good thing. But the pain seemed to come second to waiting for Hayes's call all morning. She'd reached for her cell more times to check if her ringer was turned off than she'd ever admit to anyone. But he hadn't called. And a little voice in her head told her something was very, *very* wrong.

When he finally did call, his voice had been hard and cold, telling her he wasn't alone in whatever room he sat in. "Can you and your sisters come up to Boulder? I've got something here I want to show you."

"Of course—" she had replied.

"Good. I'll see you soon."

The call ended as abruptly as it started. Maisie had felt shaken then, and that uneasiness still remained after they'd dropped Mason off at the sitter's. Only minutes into their drive to Boulder, Maisie couldn't stand being inside her own damn head with her runaway thoughts. "What do you think Hayes has found?" she asked.

Behind the driver's seat, Clara said, "Hopefully the prick that burned our trailer."

"I hope so," Amelia agreed, fingering the end of her French braid. "I don't know about all of you, but I'm beyond ready to put all this behind us and move on."

Maisie raised a hand. "I second that."

Amelia glanced back between the seats and smiled, not even saying anything about Maisie's bare feet.

How things had changed. Maisie remembered a time when Clara would've swooshed her feet off and Amelia would've have snapped that they stunk, even if they hadn't. They were kinder to one another now. Everything was so different. Not only because of Laurel's death, which ultimately had brought her closer to her sisters, but the brewery had changed them too. She realized, for the first time ever in her life, it felt like she belonged right there in the car with them. And Maisie couldn't help but wonder if that's exactly what Pops had planned all along. That his final wishes had nothing to do with the brewery itself but about bringing Maisie into Clara and Amelia's tight circle.

"Any word from the insurance adjuster?" Amelia asked, dragging Maisie from her thoughts.

Clara turned down the country song on the radio. "I talked to them this morning. He said it'd be weeks before we see any money, but I got the feeling that weeks actually means months."

"Great," Maisie grumbled, watching a hawk soaring over the hay field through her window. "I never understood why any of this takes so long. We've been paying the insurance company for years to ensure we've got money there if we need it. Why all the friggin' paperwork? Just cut the damn check."

"You won't hear me arguing," Clara said. "It's ridiculous."

Amelia agreed with a quick nod, looking ready to speak, when the GPS indicated a right turn ahead. Clara made the turn, and then Amelia looked between the seats again, a big fat grin on her face. "Now that Mason's out of the car, want to talk about what happened with Hayes and Seth last night?"

Maisie stared down at her throbbing finger in her lap. "Nothing happened with either of them."

"It didn't look like nothing to me," Amelia said, voice light. "I saw Hayes's face when he walked up and saw you dancing with Seth. He didn't look happy."

Maisie sighed, rested her head back against the headrest and looked at her sister. "Believe me when I tell you that Hayes is not jealous over Seth. I told him why Seth and I broke up, and well...he didn't like how Seth bailed. That's the reason for the tension last night."

"He's not the only one," Clara cut in. "But I've got agree with Amelia, he definitely wasn't glaring at Seth because Seth's a shitty guy."

Maisie glanced at Clara in the rearview mirror. "You saw him too?"

She nodded, and her eyes squinted a little. "Listen, I wasn't going to say anything, but I'm your older sister and keep thinking that maybe I should."

"Am I going to hate what you're about to say?" Maisie asked with caution.

Clara laughed softly. "No."

"Then proceed."

Clara's amused eyes came to Maisie's again in the rearview mirror before they softened. She pulled the car over, kicking up dust on the gravel side. On the quiet country road, Clara unhooked her seat beat. "I hope you know you don't owe anything to Hayes or Laurel."

A frown tugged on Maisie's mouth. "I don't know what you mean."

Clara turned fully in her seat. "I mean, just be happy, Maisie. You've been through so much. Far more than most people. And we saw you pick yourself up from your pain and start living again."

Amelia agreed with a soft, "You were so strong. We're so proud."

"Don't make me cry," Maisie said, pointing at Amelia.

"Won't. Promise." Amelia laughed, raising her hands in surrender.

Clara continued as if she'd never been interrupted, "I just want you to really think about why your heart reaches for Hayes. Is it because he's giving you all the happiness in the world? Or is it because you and Hayes have been through hell and back and now you feel obligated to be there for him?"

Maisie nearly answered, but then stopped herself. She did feel like she needed to be there for him. She'd been his lifeline for a while, she'd always known that, and she had no doubt Hayes knew that too.

Clara went on, "This isn't something you need to ever tell anyone, only yourself, but these are important things to ask. Because you, Maisie, with your sunny ways, deserve to be happy. Truly happy and loved."

Maisie's heart expanded, healing cracks she didn't know were there. "Thank you."

Clara smiled and nodded.

Next to her, Amelia reached for Maisie's hand, squeezing tight. "If I can add my two cents, if you do want to be with Hayes, it's okay to fall in love with him. Laurel would want you both to be happy. You both deserve a win. But, as Clara said, don't let him forget that your happiness matters too. At some point, you're going to have to stop taking care of him, and he needs to put the past behind him. And if Hayes cares about you like he should, he'd want that too."

Tears rolled down Maisie's cheeks during Amelia's speech and Maisie couldn't stop them. Love touched every broken spot in her heart. This felt really nice. "Thanks," she said with a sniff. "I actually think I'm finally starting to think of myself again." And maybe she hadn't seen that before. Just how lost she'd become. How much of herself she'd given up after Laurel died. Because seeing Seth shifted something inside her last night, reminding her of all the things Maisie had wanted for herself... before Laurel died, before Pops died, before the brewery.

Clara smiled and gave Maisie's hand another tight squeeze. "Good, I'm glad, and if you need anything from us while you figure this out, you'll let us know."

"I will," Maisie said. "I love you both. Thank you."

"Love you back, Maisie-Moo," Amelia said, eyes watery too.

Clara gave a soft smile and mouthed *"love you"* before she fastened her seat belt again drove off.

They passed buzzards gathering at the side of the road, and Maisie's head began to hurt as much as her finger. She wasn't going to get any answers in the car right now. To get her mind off herself, she aimed the spotlight on Amelia. "Since you're in the talking mood, how about we talk about your fight with Luka, and Beckett getting growly about it?"

Amelia went still. "I've got nothing to say about that."

"Sure, you don't." Clara snickered, elbowing Amelia next to her. "What should we talk about, then?"

Amelia turned her sly grin on Clara. "How about that guy you were kissing?"

Clara swerved the car, the tires hitting gravel before she straightened the car on the road.

"Oh, damn, you near drove off of the road," Maisie drawled. "This has got to be good."

Clara straightened in her seat, her cheeks burning red. "No one was supposed to see that." Her stern eyes flicked to Amelia. "How did you see that?"

"You weren't exactly hiding it," Amelia said with a snort. "You were just too busy to notice that your hiding spot sucked."

Clara's shoulders curled. "Oh my God."

Maisie burst out laughing.

Amelia glanced back at Maisie and nodded. "You should have seen our big sis here. It was scandalous. She practically ate the guy's face off then grabbed him by the T-shirt and dragged him into the storage room."

Maisie gasped jokingly, a hand on her heart. "Oh my."

Clara frowned at Maisie in the rearview mirror. "All right, that's enough. So, I had some fun last night."

"I'm just busting your balls," Maisie said with an answering grin. "Or did you bust his balls?"

"Just stop," Clara muttered.

Amelia laughed then quieted enough to ask, "Who was he anyway?"

"I have no idea, and that's exactly how I like it."

Maisie whistled. "Look at you, being all...wild."

Clara straightened her shoulders and replied, "Mason's the only one I'm thinking about right now, but last night was some much-needed fun."

"You don't need to explain yourself," Maisie countered. "You deserve all the screwing in the barn you want."

Amelia burst out laughing again.

Clara muttered something incoherent under her breath.

Maisie just looked back out the window and did what she totally didn't expect today, she smiled.

🐚

Hayes stood at the coffeemaker in the break room in the Boulder police department and made himself coffee. He stared out at the cops in the police station, much larger than River Rock. Beat cops, detectives, special units, the station was a flurry of activity with all the cops working as a solid team. He'd accepted his father's offer, diving in headfirst to solve Maisie's case. Now that the case was solved, Hayes's mind slowed down, processed this new direction of his life, and exactly how he wanted things to unfold from this day forward.

"Maisie Carter is here to see you."

Hayes glanced over his shoulder at Neil. "Thanks."

"No problem," Neil said. "Let me know when you're done."

"Will do." Hayes grabbed his coffee and headed out of the breakroom, immediately spotting Maisie through the window in the waiting room. One look at her and he wanted to take her into his arms, hold there tight, and yet...*and yet,* he didn't want to make a wrong move. Hurt her. "Hey," he said, by way of greeting.

In the empty waiting room, all three sisters were on their feet, eyes filled with curiosity. But Maisie spoke first, "Is everything okay?" she asked.

He nodded, and with his free hand, he took out three badges from his pocket. "I've already got you signed in. Clip these on."

Maisie accepted hers, clipping the badge onto her shirt, while her sisters did the same. "Okay, now the suspense is killing me," Maisie quipped. "Quit with the cop look and fess up. What's going on?"

Hayes was mid-turn but stopped, glancing back at her with an arched brow. "The cop look?"

"Yeah, all broody and blank, not giving away anything."

He couldn't fight the chuckle that escaped him, regardless that he could all but taste the tension between them. "I'm not exactly sure if that's a good thing or bad, but we've found the perpetrator in your case."

"That fucker," Amelia snapped.

Hayes nodded at her. "That about sums it up, but I've got good news too. We've found all your equipment."

Maisie gaped. "The stuff from the festival?"

"Yeah, we found it all."

Clara beamed. "That is great news. Thank you so much."

He inclined his head, gesturing for them to follow. "It surprised the shit out of me too," he said, leading them down the hallway. "But in the chop-shop they worked out of, we found it all there. The jockey box, the sign, the bottle openers, and buttons. Kegs were empty though."

"Guess they're fans of our beer, huh?" Maisie joked.

Hayes smiled at her. "Seems like it."

He pushed open the door at the end of the hallway and

Maisie gasped. "Wow, you weren't lying." She scanned the area from left to right, her gaze touching on all the things she thought she'd lost. "It's all here. I thought it was all burned."

That relief on her face drew him in deep. He became desperate to pull her close. To inhale her scent, which always told him everything was going to be okay. But where would that get them? Him leaning on her, depending on her, when she needed the exact opposite.

Last night, he'd made a promise to himself. Fix everything. One step then another. No more winging life. Clara had been spot on, and those words shook him to his core. Maisie deserved to be loved in the way she loved others. Just when that thought clawed at him, he forced his thoughts to clear, staying focused on the current task. "From what the suspect said," Hayes said to the sisters, "they removed anything of value from the trailer. The tires, engine, stuff like that. Then they burned what they didn't need and tried to obscure the VIN and fingerprints before they took it to a junkyard."

"Well, it worked," Clara pointed out.

Hayes nodded and tucked his free hand in his pocket, sipping his coffee. When the bitter brew hit his tongue, he swallowed quickly then asked no one in particular, "Do you want to see him?"

All eyes went to Clara. She shook her head adamantly. "I don't."

"Me neither," Amelia said, scrunching her nose.

Not unexpectedly, Maisie said, "I'd like to."

Hayes nodded to her and then said to Amelia and Clara, "Feel free to start putting this stuff in your car. Whatever doesn't fit, I can take home in my truck. We won't be long."

"Sounds good," Clara said. "And thanks, Hayes, for everything."

She still held a question in her gaze. One he didn't blame her for one bit. She was protecting her baby sister. Hayes simply inclined his head in acknowledgment, and Clara began to gather the boxes.

"Just this way," Hayes said, settling his hand low on Maisie's back and guiding her toward the door.

Down another hallway and through a door on the right, she stopped in front of a one-way mirror. "That's him?" Maisie said, examining the lanky teenager through the window.

Hayes shut the door tight, then sidled next to her. "Yup."

"He looks so young," she said, staring at the kid sitting at the metal table, shaking in his boots. "How old is he?"

"He's seventeen."

Maisie's concerned eyes came to Hayes. "Jeez, he's just a kid. How did you find him?"

"We caught him on the security footage."

"*We* or *you*?" Maisie asked.

Hayes leaned a shoulder against the glass and arched an eyebrow. "Does it matter?"

"Of course, it matters," she said, stepping closer, bringing all that sunniness into his space. "I need to know who I should thank."

"These things are always a team effort," he told her. Needing her, against his better judgment he moved in closer, hugged her tight and pressed his lips on the top of head. "Can I come see you tomorrow? We need to talk."

She leaned away and gave him a sweet smile. "We don't need to talk. I'm okay."

Which was the fucking point. Clara wasn't wrong. Maisie deserved better, but she was so damn loving she'd wait for the conversation she deserved until *he* was ready. That didn't sit well. Not anymore. "We'll talk tomorrow," he repeated.

She visibly swallowed. "Okay." Then she loosed a breath and stepped back, looking back at the kid. "Tell them not to be too hard on him."

"He stole your trailer and burned it," he gently reminded her.

Tenderness crossed her face. "Yeah, he did, but I actually think his actions forced me to think differently. His actions are the very thing that might lead to my happiness." She moved closer again, stood on her tiptoes and pressed a soft kiss to his mouth. "I'll see you later."

Then she was gone.

But what she said wasn't gone. The words echoed in his head, weaving their way down into his tight chest while he drove back to River Rock. *Might lead to my happiness...* If anyone should have happiness hand delivered to them, it was Maisie Carter.

After he entered the station, he caught his father in his office. Hayes knocked on the door. His father's head snapped up. "All done?" Dad asked.

"Yeah, the kid's been processed." Hayes tapped the file folder in his hands. "Got some paperwork but shouldn't take long."

"Good."

Hayes moved to the seat across from his dad and sat, looking down at his clenched fists. For the past week, his thoughts were a loud roar in his ears, every question more confusing than the last. Until it finally occurred to him today that he could never go back. He couldn't change a damn thing about his past. And maybe it was time to stop fighting that.

Dad's voice softened. "Are you waiting for me to say something, son?"

"I can't give you six months," Hayes said, forcing the words out of his dry throat. He looked up at his father, whose head was cocked. "With all that's happened, all that has gone wrong, I need roots that extend past six months." Because he couldn't live like he had been. Day to day, hoping and praying he'd survive the next one.

He *had* survived. And so had Maisie.

Sitting behind his desk, Dad steepled his fingers, his eyes searching Hayes's. "Then tell me what you want."

The answer, for how much of a struggle it had been to find it, suddenly became clear. He gestured at the file folders for new applicants on his father's desk. "Is one of those available positions you've got for a detective?"

Dad gave a slow nod. "One of them, yes."

"Before—" Hayes cleared the emotion clogging his throat, forcing himself to go on. "In the months before we lost Laurel, I had been told that I could take my detective test in Denver. Obviously, that plan was thwarted. But I've got the bachelor's degree in criminal justice and the work history behind me."

"You do," Dad agreed. "Is that what you're thinking? You want to be a detective?"

Hayes let all the guards down, showing his father all his weak spots. "I've been on the side of a victim. I need to be back on the other side."

"I think that makes sense," Dad said gently.

Hayes loosed a breath, tension melting away. "I can't go back to being a beat cop, getting behind a cruiser, living the same life I did with Laurel."

"You need something new? Something different?" A

wide smile spread across Dad's face. "Something you're very good at."

Hayes nodded. "No taking it easy on me. I earn my way, like everyone else."

Dad snorted, leaning against his chair to fold him arms. "I don't know why you always thought I was throwing a job at you. Because you're my son, you'll need to work ten times harder."

Hayes didn't reply, simply glad for it. It occurred to him then that he didn't have to transfer to Denver all those years ago, in fear that his father would make it easy on him. He was glad the bar was set high. It would make him work to reach it. He rose and moved to the door. There, he squeezed the doorjamb and glanced over his shoulder. "Did you always know I'd come back to the force?"

"I hoped." Dad's expression went utterly soft, as did his voice, a rare thing for his father. "You're a cop, Hayes, through and through, and I'm glad you remembered that." His gaze shifted back to his papers then, dismissing Hayes. "Now go home and study your ass off. If you fail your test, you'll have to answer to me."

Hayes chuckled and left his office, finally feeling like he'd taken the right step forward.

15

L ater that night, Maisie sat on her bed, sketching
her memory of that day at the stream with Hayes.
Soft, instrumental music played from her cell on
the bedside table. Her small bedside lamp was turned on, a
soft yellowish light warming the space. She'd taken some
strong painkillers an hour ago, and with her finger finally
pain-free, she had grabbed her sketch pad. Drawing
awkwardly, but making it work, she let her pencil flow easily
over the page, not exactly sure if she was getting the drawing
right, but the stream, the mossy rocks, even Hayes sitting
there, it all flowed from her pencil to the page. And creating
something was keeping her mind off the fact that Hayes
wanted to talk. She couldn't explain why, but things
felt...*different*. He felt different. And she wasn't quite sure
about any of it.

"Look at this."

Maisie glanced away from her page, finding Clara
barging into her room. "What is it?"

"Just look." Clara offered the phone.

Maisie read the Google search, scanned the news articles, not believing what she saw before her. *Great beer. Fun times. Three Chicks Brewery Outshines the Competition.* "Holy shit," she breathed.

"Yeah, holy shit is right," Clara said, accepting her phone back. "You did that, Maisie. You know that, right? You pulled off something that even I hadn't thought possible. You not only fixed the problem with missing that last festival, you blew our competition away. We went from a thousand followers on social media to over twenty thousand. Us. A small little brewery in River Rock." Clara tucked her phone away in the pocket of her jeans and then took Maisie by the shoulders, squeezing gently. "*You* did that, just being you, creating in the way you do. I'm really, really proud of you, Maisie. Pops would have been too."

"Thanks." Maisie smiled, and yet somehow that happiness couldn't quite reach her heart.

"And the best news yet," Clara added, releasing Maisie's shoulders to take a seat on the bed. "Today a distributor contacted me."

"Shut up!" Maisie gasped.

"It's true," Clara said with a laugh. "I'm going into Denver for a meeting in a week." Clara shook her head, obviously not believing all this either. "I didn't even have to call them, Maisie. They called me. I hope you feel really good about this."

"I do," Maisie said. "Hell, I actually feel like I've gotten something right for once."

Clara gave an understanding nod and then took Maisie's good hand, squeezing tight. "Listen, you've done your part here, and I know that's been important to you. Doing this for us. For Pops. But it's okay, you know, if you want to branch out now, and see what else is out there for you. We all know that the brewery isn't really your thing, and definitely not satisfying you, so here's your chance, Maisie. Go do what makes your heart happy."

Maisie lowered her gaze to their held hands. "You won't be disappointed?"

"How could I be?" Clara countered. "You did your part. You've got no reason to feel like you're leaving us hanging. Of course, it would be ideal if you wait to pull out your one-third in the company until we've gotten more successful, but if you absolutely need it, we'll find a way to make it work with a loan or something." She tucked a finger under Maisie's chin, until Maisie lifted her eyes. "You got me an in with a distributor. Now it's my turn to take the brewery to the next level. You're an artist, a dreamer. Go create, sprinkle your sunshine where it's most needed. Whenever we have big parties at the brewery, you can take control of those. You'll always be a part of the brewery, if you want to be."

Maisie nearly parted her lips and said *thank you, yes, I totally want this*, but one thing stopped her. "There's a lot going on right now in my life, and not only professionally. I don't think it's a good time to make any huge decisions."

Clara smiled and patted the top of Maisie's hand. "That's probably the most mature thing I've ever heard you say." She rose and placed a kiss on Maisie's forehead. "You don't need to rush anything, just take a little time, all right, figure out what makes you happy. You deserve that."

When Clara reached the door, Maisie called, "I'm not the only one who deserves to be happy, you know."

Clara's smile softened, but before she could respond, a ball of energy suddenly burst into the room. Mason jumped, literally like a monkey, on her bed. Maisie snatched him up and smothered him with kisses.

"Ew," Mason snapped, fighting to get away. "Stop kissing me, Auntie Maisie."

"Never," she said, pulling him in and kissing him again. "You're just so loveable."

Mason wiggled out of her reach, bounced on the bed again and then took off out of the room.

Clara shook her head at her son. "Well, that's one way to get him out of here quick." She laughed and shut the door behind her.

The clock on the bedside table read 8:30, Mason's normal bedtime, and Maisie heard the old pipes complain when Clara turned on the faucet for his bath. Desperate to get lost in her sketch, instead of her tangled thoughts, she turned back to her drawing, unaware of how much time passed when there was a knock on her bedroom door. "Come in," she called.

The door opened, revealing Penelope and Amelia on the other side, both wearing Yoga pants and T-shirts, typical girls' night in clothing. Penelope was holding a pie and a bottle of wine. Amelia had three forks and wine glasses. All indicating that Clara must have called in reinforcements when Maisie's sunshine wasn't shining as bright tonight.

"We come bearing butter pecan deliciousness," Penelope said, holding up the pie like a prized possession.

"Then you may enter," Maisie said, and patted her bed.

She set her drawing aside on the bedside table, but Amelia caught sight of it as she slid onto the bed across from her. "Wow. That's really gorgeous," Amelia said. "Is that Hayes?"

Maisie nodded, dropping her pencil next to the drawing. "Yup. It's a little rough because of the finger, but I'll polish it up once the splint comes off."

"Doesn't look rough at all to me, but then again, I can't even draw a stick person well," Penelope said, sitting cross-legged at the end of the bed and accepting the fork from

Amelia before pointing it at Maisie. "All right, girl, we've got pie and wine, and you totally killed it last night. You should be really happy right now, but you look really, really sad. What's up?"

Maisie accepted the fork from Amelia and took a big bite of the pie. Her taste buds exploded with delight at the sugary sweetness before she answered Penelope. "My head is just...messy."

"It can't be that messy," Penelope said. "Try and explain."

Maisie inhaled deeply and blew it out just as slow. "I don't know, I mean... When things began happening with Hayes, I asked him if we'd complicated things by sleeping together, and he said no."

Amelia asked, "But it's suddenly gotten complicated?"

"Complicated, yeah," Maisie said with a shrug. "It's just tense now, when it wasn't tense before. I'm not exactly sure what's going on with him, but something's going on."

Penelope swallowed a of sip wine and then asked, "Have you tried talking to him about it?"

"Of course, but he just shuts me out saying nothing is wrong." Maisie dug her fork back into the pie, gobbling up the sugary goodness. "When I went to see Luna, she said he's keeping a secret."

Penelope cocked her head. "What secret would he be keeping?"

"I don't know," Maisie said, voicing the same thought she'd had over and over again. "But the more I think about it, and the way he's been distant, maybe it's that he can't feel for me what I feel for him. And maybe he feels guilty about that, because after all we've been through, he should want to make me happy, but he can't because his heart belongs to Laurel. I mean, maybe that's it?"

"But Hayes cares about you so much," Amelia countered. "Everyone can see that."

Maisie acknowledged that with a nod. "Yes, but maybe it's a platonic, just friends, type of thing, but he didn't realize that until it was too late. Now he doesn't want to say anything, too afraid he'll hurt my feelings."

Penelope snorted. "You've had sex with him. It can't be platonic, babe."

"Okay, true," Maisie hedged, "but maybe he was just using me to blow off steam though, you know? Like he needed that release or something."

"Which he could have had with anyone." Amelia stuck her fork in the pie, cutting off a small piece. "I doubt he'd cross the friendship line with you if there weren't something there. Did it feel disconnected, like *just sex*?"

Maisie slowly shook her head. "No, it felt like more."

Amelia paused, chewing on her pie and then offered, "Well, I say there's no sense beating around the bush anymore. Ask him straight out what he's keeping from you."

"Did that," Maisie replied. "And he said he's not keeping any secrets."

Penelope asked, "Did you believe him?"

"No."

Heavy silence filled the room. The type of silence that came from simply having no answers to a thousand questions.

Penelope finally broke the heavy silence, "What exactly does that mean for you two, then?"

"I don't know." Maisie shrugged. "He said he wants to talk tomorrow. One way or the other, I'll hopefully get some clarity."

Amelia studied Maisie. "As hard as it is, maybe it's time to let go of Hayes. You've had your heart set on him for a long time. Take Seth last night. He's hot and available, and was totally eating you up."

"But there is a big problem with that," Maisie said.

Penelope asked, "Which is?"

"My heart doesn't want Seth." Maisie stuck the fork back in the pie. "It only wants Hayes."

Hayes wasn't sure what had woken him during the night or how he ended up at his back door, but he stepped out into the fog in his backyard. The willow tree hemmed a meandering creek at the edge of his property. He recalled going for a run after talking with his father to burn off the shit going on his head before talking to Maisie tomorrow. But he couldn't remember how he got *here*. The wet earth infused the air as he stepped onto the dewy grass, the soft squish of mud moving beneath his bare feet. Hayes strode absent-mindedly toward the creek, pulled there by a force he couldn't see but could feel. When he reached the creek, he noticed the rippling water slipping over wet stones, partially submerged twigs in the water, drifting leaves and air bubbles floating lazily downstream. But his attention shifted when he realized he wasn't alone. The blond-haired beauty next to him, with the soft green eyes, and fair features, was no stranger. "Laurel?"

She smiled, wearing the same white nightgown she'd been wearing when he'd found her in their bedroom. Her blond hair was pulled back in a braid, strands free around her face.

"Surprised to see me?"

He blinked, but she remained. "How is this possible?"

She offered her hand. "You know, you don't always have to have the answers for everything."

But he needed answers. He needed logic, and nothing about this was logical. Everything slowed around him when he took her delicate fingers in his. She felt solid, so familiar. "You feel warm."

"You'd expect different?" she asked with a laugh, leading him closer to the tree where he'd spread her ashes.

The world spun away from him as he glanced down to their intertwined hands. He sat next to her under the tree and she felt *real*. Like she'd never left him. "This can't be real."

She tightened her fingers. "This doesn't feel real to you?"

"It does," he countered, losing himself in the tight way she held him. "But..."

Laurel gazed at the creek and then up at the willow tree. "I like it here. You picked a good place for me to rest."

His mind wanted to refuse this as truth. He decided to stop fighting, needing to get all the things he wanted to say out. "It felt right when I found this place. You would have been happy living here. We should have moved here. You would have been safe."

She turned to him with a smile that broke his chest wide open. "I would have loved this house, you're right." Her gaze fell to the home behind him. "But this was never meant to be my home."

He sucked in a harsh breath, the world feeling like it was slipping away from him. "It should have been."

She gave a dry laugh. "Should have, could have, might have, those are all possibilities that will never be."

His stomach roiled. He'd been saying those statements for far too long. To ground himself, prove this was truly happening, he looked out at the pebbles and gravel half-buried in the muddy creek bottom. She moved closer, leaned her head against his shoulder, and said, "You know why I'm here. You know what we have to talk about."

Hayes shut his eyes against the exposed wound in his heart. "What if I don't want to talk?" He enveloped her, holding her tight to him. "What if I just want to keep you like this and not let you go away again?"

"We don't get that choice, but choose if you're ever going to forgive yourself."

"How can I?" he said, time seemingly halting. "It's my fault you disappeared."

Laurel leaned away from him. Her gaze was sharp like it used to be when she got annoyed with him. "You're looking at this all wrong."

"How else am I supposed to look at it? I let someone live, and that choice cost your life."

She placed her hand on his arm, a warm, touching comfort that seemed familiar. "The alternative would have been that you killed an unarmed man. That's not you. That won't ever be you."

"But if I had, you'd still be here," he said.

She slowly shook her head. "I'm not supposed to be here. Nothing you could have done would have changed that. Maybe the manner of how I died might have changed, but I would have gone, regardless."

"I don't believe that."

She laughed softly. "Not even you can change what's written in the stars, Hayes."

He wanted to shout that he could fix all this. Make it all right again, but control had been lost to him a long time ago. Water trickled around rocks and over twigs. Everything was too vivid. Too real. "Were you afraid...when it happened?"

She shook her head. "No. I didn't feel anything. Didn't hear anything. It happened so fast."

His eyes welled. He blinked to clear his eyesight, only to make sure he kept seeing her. "It didn't hurt?"

"Nothing hurt."

Hayes gathered her in his arms, just for this second. He held on tight, having no idea how much time he'd get. "Did you wonder if I'd come?"

"It all happened too fast for any of that, Hayes," she explained gently. "You have to stop blaming yourself. Don't waste any more time. Be happy. If not for you, for her."

He knew exactly who she was talking about. "Maisie."

Laurel leaned away and smiled bright, the deep love for Maisie shining in her expression. "You're nearly there. So close to having what life is all about. People. Family. Friends. Love. It's all that matters, Hayes. If you want to do right by me, then forgive yourself for you, forgive yourself for her. Be happy. Be good to her. Be good to each other."

Hayes shut his eyes, feeling Laurel's pulsating energy next to him, swearing she was right there. Her floral perfume smelled the same. The press of her head on his shoulder was so familiar. The words she said, all the things he knew she'd say to him. Warmth began to fill the broken, cold, dead parts of his heart. Somewhere in his mind, he knew this couldn't be real, but his heart didn't listen.

"I miss you," he told her, holding her close. "We both miss you so much."

She met him with teary eyes. "I miss you and Maisie too."

He caught those tears and wiped them away. "I could have saved you, if I'd only gotten there in time."

"No, Hayes, you couldn't," she said, closing the distance until her arms were around him tight. "Stop slowly dying for

me. I never wanted that. If you do anything now, *live* for me."
Then her smile warmed. "Make Maisie's dreams come true.
All of them. You and only you can do this for her."

Hayes's chest tightened. "I wanted your dreams to come
true too."

"They did," Laurel said. "I had you. I had Maisie. I had
everything I ever wanted and more."

"You didn't have time."

She lifted her hand to his face. "Move forward. It's time
for that."

Her voice became distant, her warmth slowly dissipat-
ing, replaced by a cold void Hayes couldn't run from. He
wanted to scream, to run to her, but suddenly, his eyes
snapped open.

Shadows spread across his ceiling. "Fuck," he breathed,
sitting up, drenched in sweat, thrusting his hands in his hair.
It'd all been a dream, or his subconscious, but his feet were
moving anyway. When he reached the back door, he flung it
open, not sure what he'd find.

The early morning was just the same. The fog. The wet
earth. The quiet. He shut his eyes, swearing he could still
feel Laurel right there. But when he opened them, he was
alone.

16

A *ping* on Maisie's window jolted her awake. The clock read 5:02. She slid out of bed, quickly moving to her window. She was completely unprepared when she realized Hayes had thrown a pebble at her window. She opened the window before he could throw another one. "What are you doing?" she called down to him.

He stood near the porch light, the morning fog hanging over the wet earth. He wore a T-shirt and jogging pants, his hair a wild mess. Obviously he'd either not slept yet or had just woken up. "We need to talk," he called up to her.

She leaned out the window. "Now? I thought we were meeting later?"

"I couldn't wait. I didn't want to ring the doorbell and wake everyone up, and you're not answering your phone." She always silenced the ringer at bedtime. "Open the window all the way, I'm coming up."

"You're coming up," she repeated, then gaped at him. "Seriously?"

He hopped up on the porch's railing, climbed the pillar

and then hoisted himself up onto the roof. Maisie's heart raced a little bit faster the closer he got. Admittedly, this little stunt fulfilled some teenage fantasy she'd once written about in her diary.

When he reached her, she stepped aside and he climbed through the window, which she closed after him. She turned to him as he moved to her bed. "I've got to say this is probably the most romantic gesture anyone has ever made for me." He sat down on the bed and then his eyes met hers, and her smile faded at the darkness in their depths, the emptiness there. "What's wrong?"

"We need to talk."

Her heart dropped into the pit of her stomach. She wanted to move to him, comfort him, and yet, her feet wouldn't move her there, stuck in the worry that what he was going to say would ruin everything. "Okay. Then talk."

He shut his eyes thrust his hands in his hair, bowed his head. "This is...this isn't easy for me."

The despondent tone of his voice. The shaking of his hands. The curl of his shoulders. She sat on her bed next to him and took his trembling hand. "Hayes, it's me. Talk."

He kept his head bowed, looking smaller than she could ever imagine he could. "I killed Laurel."

She blinked, a cold bite hitting her stomach. "I don't understand what just came out of your mouth."

"I wasn't the one who pulled the trigger, but I was the reason Laurel got shot. What you don't know is, I was working gang crime in Denver. We had a big bust, but I shot the leader in the shoulder, instead of killing him, because I wanted him to be put to justice for the crime wave he spread across Denver." Hayes gave Maisie a quick look and then averted his gaze again, his voice trembling. "That leader went after Laurel in retribution."

Her head spun. "But they said it was a robbery gone wrong?"

"The gang's involvement was kept out of the media because of the ongoing investigation, and because we didn't want to spread more fear." Maisie gripped her middle as he went on. "I hate myself for it. I wish I could go back and take that shot again. Or get there in time to protect her."

Maisie felt the ground drop out from under her. She forced the words out of her dry throat. "Is this why you walked away from being a cop?"

His nod was slow, and he looked so very tired. "*I* am the reason she is dead." His voice had never sounded so empty, so full of shame. "I was supposed to protect innocent lives, and I put a bull's-eye on my wife's back. I didn't protect her. I failed her. I failed you by taking away your best friend. I failed everyone, including my honor to the badge."

Tears flooded her eyes, coldness seeping into all the warm spots in her soul. She heard every desolate word that came out of his mouth, but she realized that, even with the shame he carried, he'd done the unthinkable days ago. He'd ignored his pain, his shame, his fear, and went back to the job to protect Maisie. To right a wrong in her life. "Is this what you were keeping from me?"

"I didn't protect her," he barely whispered. "I was worried you'd hate me. That I'd break your heart all over again by telling you this. But deep down, I'm also scared that I won't be able to protect you if the time comes. I can't lose you, Maisie."

He thought he'd failed Laurel. That he'd fail Maisie too. Her heart broke for him as she cupped his face and forced him to look at her. Tears were in his eyes, and that pain slowed time around her. "Hayes, my God, is this what you've been carrying with you all this time?"

His voice blistered. "It's the truth—"

"No," she snapped, unable to control the raw emotion fueling her voice. "It's not the truth. This is a lie that your pain has told you. Laurel's death isn't your fault. The man you shot in the street did that to her."

"But I—" She placed a hand over his mouth.

"You need to listen to me now," she said firmly. "I refuse to let you live another day thinking that you've somehow caused this. You did not cause Laurel's death."

He shut his eyes.

"Look at me, Hayes," she snapped. He opened his eyes to the tears in hers. "This is not your fault. You didn't put a bull's-eye on Laurel's back. An evil person hunted her. And if I have to tell you that every fucking day for the rest of my life until you believe me, then that's exactly what I'm going to do."

He placed his hands over hers on his face. "For the rest of your life?"

"Yes. For the rest of my life." She tightened her hands. "We didn't go through all this to have you hate yourself for something you couldn't control. Don't let him win like that."

Raw emotion bled in his gaze as his expression turned warm and attentive on *her*. "If it weren't for you, I don't know where I would have ended up. You picked me up when I couldn't get off the ground. You stayed right there when any other sane person would have walked away. You breathed life back into me." Her breath hitched, and tears rained down her cheeks at the truth he'd never said. He swiped her tears away and went on roughly, "I'm not sure I'll ever achieve it, but damn will I try to show you that kind of love back."

She took in every word he said. She rose up on her

knees, closing the space between them. "Hayes Taylor, are you telling me that you love me?"

The corners of his mouth curved. He brushed his thumbs across her cheeks. "Maisie Carter, of course I love you."

"Well," she said, warmth radiating out of her chest, "it's about damn time you admit it, because I love you too."

His mouth sealed over hers, and all the things she didn't know about Hayes suddenly blended into one truth. Somehow, against all the odds, against all the pain, against all the misery, they found a way through the darkness of grief and made it out on the other side. That wound would remain, bleeding with guilt, but she'd help heal it.

When urgency overtook all the raw emotion, they ripped at each other's clothes until he lifted her onto the bed and covered her body with is. Bare beneath him, there was nothing between them now. No more dark lie causing Hayes to keep his distance. No more fears pulling him away. His heart was bared to her, and she held it tight.

"I want to feel you," he said, pressing a kiss near her ear, his hardened length stroking over her wet sex. "Are you protected?"

"I'm on the pill." Breathless, she angled her chin, allowing his access. "No STIs either."

"I'm safe too." His head lifted, gaze locked onto her. Emotion and rawness lived in those eyes. *Love.* Every single part of her soul, he knew; the darkest of the dark; every weak spot, and every great and strong one too. And she knew his, felt all of him now.

Locked in his smoldering eyes, he lifted his hips, placing his tip at her entrance, waiting for permission. She slid her legs up around his hips and guided him deep inside her. She moaned. He groaned. And if he planned on saying something else, those words died as he slid in and out, a low growl ruminating from deep in his throat, pushing all of him inside her.

She lost herself in the pleasure when his hand pressed to her hip, pinning her to the mattress while he worked her in long, slow strokes. She explored the flexing muscles of his shoulders when he sealed his mouth over hers in a move so possessive, she felt all the unknowns, all the questions about them, immediately disappear. He couldn't get any closer, keeping himself pressed against her, his weight leaning on his arms as each thrust became harder and faster. She squeezed harder, desperate to keep him in. Because this wasn't just sex. With them, it was always more.

"You've got me, Maisie," he whispered against her mouth. "All of me."

"Yes," she breathed. "I love you, Hayes."

He kissed her cheek, her neck, then brushed against her ear. "I love you."

He had a point to make, and he made it. One hard thrust after another. Each one sending her back arching and her toes curling as his pelvis fed pleasure to her clit, along with the thick hardness driving inside her, making her feel perfectly full of his love.

That's when she froze, wanting this to last a lifetime. Right there, in this bliss with him. But then she was falling into this new place. A safe place. A happy place. A feeling she'd chase again and again, and this time, locked together, he went with her.

17

Two weeks later, early on a Saturday, Hayes's suggestion to spend the morning downtown turned into an impromptu trip to the farmer's market. Maisie caught the sizzle of meat and the vendors calling out to customers. She had dragged him into the market before he even knew where she was going. In the park on Main Street, Maisie passed by the rows of tables and booths filled with local, seasonal produce. Off in the distance, the Rocky Mountains and their snowy peaks stood high.

"What about steaks and zucchini for dinner?" Hayes asked, his gaze on the produce booth.

"Yes, and yes." She smiled.

He dropped a quick kiss on her lips. "I'll catch up."

"Okay."

With him moving toward the booth, Maisie kept walking ahead, drawn by the floral scent coming from the roses and lavender ahead of her. Two weeks had gone by since the party at the brewery, and she still didn't exactly know where she was going to go from here. She knew she'd done her part to push the brewery ahead and help them stand out in the crowd of craft breweries in Colorado. Clara had given her a way out to find her own path now, whatever that may be. She'd be crazy not to take it. And yet...*and yet* what else was she going to do? A handful of part-time jobs to make ends meet wasn't satisfying anymore, and as much as she loved throwing the parties at the brewery, and would continue to do so, she needed something...more.

The thought stayed with her as she stopped by the booth with the fresh flowers. "I'll take a dozen of the daisies, please." Her absolute favorite.

"Wonderful choice." The lady behind the table began packing them up.

Warmth and strength engulfed Maisie, and quite possibly the yummiest cologne known to man, as Hayes wrapped his arms around her from behind. "I love that, in a farmer's market, you go straight to the flowers."

"Why, what's wrong with buying flowers?" she asked, leaning back into him.

"Nothing wrong with it, but I think it's sweet you always gravitate to all the beautiful things." He kissed her neck and said softly in her ear, "You just can't help it."

She smiled and stayed there for a minute. Just being happy. They deserved that.

When the lady brought the bundle of flowers over, Maisie paid for them. "Thanks."

"Enjoy the lovely day," the woman said with a smile.

They carried on through the market, striding by the booth with the woodsy scent from the smoky cured meats when Hayes asked, "Can I show you something? It's not far from here."

She noted the twinkle in his eyes. "Am I in for a surprise?"

He hemmed and hawed a little, and then he gave a big, bright smile. One that Maisie hadn't seen in a very long time. "I'd say that's a definite yes."

She grinned in return and linked arms with him. "Then yes, you know I love a good surprise."

Soon, they left the crowded market behind, making it back onto Main Street. People flooded downtown on Saturdays, not only for the market, but for all the quaint little shops the downtown had to offer. They strode past a food truck, and Maisie's mouth watered at the greasy aroma flowing out in the air. A look at the giant burger with overflowing cheese had her turning toward Hayes. "We need to come back here for lunch before we go home."

Hayes followed her gaze and nodded. "Agreed. Come on, let's cross the road." He headed toward the curb, and with her arm linked with his, she followed. Once they crossed safely, he continued, "You've successfully finished the festivals, regardless of the obstacles. You pierced a certain guy's heart with one of your arrows. You also helped that guy realize he needed to go back to his law enforcement roots."

"I sure did," she replied.

Hayes smiled gently down at her. "What comes next for Maisie Carter?"

She'd wondered that herself over and over again for the past week. "Good question. I haven't exactly figured that out yet."

He arched an eyebrow. "But the brewery? You're done with that?"

She laughed dryly. "It would be stupid of me not to get out when I can. I mean, really, it's amazing that it all turned out okay, but my heart isn't in working there. Everyone knows that. I've actually made something happen there and gave Clara what she needed for this next step. I don't want to push my luck." But she'd leave her inheritance in the brewery for now. Pops wanted that, and she wanted her sisters to succeed. Just because she didn't want to work full-time at the brewery didn't mean she couldn't help out and still support it. The business belonged to the Carter sisters. That would never change, no matter what.

The sides of Hayes's mouth curved a little. He stopped in the middle of the sidewalk and gestured to a little shop set in between a tea shop and an ice cream parlor. The shop was empty now, but before it had been a cute chocolate shop that made incredible candied apples. "I bet your dreams lie here, though."

She stared at the antique black door and the white-and-black striped awning overhead. "Here?" she repeated.

Warmth and emotion filled his eyes, making her belly flip-flop. "I bought this shop for you."

"You...*what*?" She gasped. Blinked. And blinked again. "How? I mean, why? Wait...*what*?"

He laughed loudly and laced his fingers with hers, holding tight. "When Laurel passed away, I was given her insurance policy money. I used it to buy the house with the willow tree because I wanted a place for Laurel to rest, a spot just for her at her favorite tree."

When Hayes spread Laurel's ashes, she'd cried in his arms, and he'd cried too. "Okay...?"

Hayes continued, "I hadn't used all of the money, though. I didn't want to spend it on myself. I thought about donating it, but something always stopped me. I finally know why now. It's because I'm supposed to use the money for this. For you. For your art studio."

Tears welled, her voice shaking. "Hayes," she barely managed. "I can't let you do that."

"I didn't do anything," he said, his voice trembling too.

"This is Laurel's last gift to you. She would have wanted this for you. For you to be happy. To make all your dreams come true."

Maisie burst into tears, and Hayes had her in his arms a second later, holding her tight.

A long time after, he eventually said, with a thick voice, "I thought this would make you happy."

"I am happy," she sobbed, leaning away to wipe away her tears. "So happy. I can't believe you did this for me." The dreams she once had felt like were right *there,* so close she could almost reach them. She glanced back at the store, seeing all the possibilities. Art lessons. Paint nights. Selling her art. She could pour all of herself into this place. "I'll pay you back, I promise."

"That's not necessary."

She turned back to him and then nearly fell over.

Hayes was down on one knee, a black little box in his hand, revealing a stunning flower-shaped diamond ring. "We could draw this out. Do the dating thing. But for years, you've carried me through the darkest time of my life. It's time we make our mark on this world, you and I. Together. Maisie, will you marry me?"

"Yes," she gasped. "Of course, Hayes. Yes, I'll marry you!"

He slid the ring on her finger. A perfect fit. Sudden applause surrounded them as Hayes gathered her in his arms. His woodsy cologne infused the air when he sealed his mouth across hers and kissed her like no one was watching.

When she leaned away, she stared into her past, her present, and her future. "Do you think Laurel would be happy for us?" she asked.

A knowing glint twinkled in his eyes. "Yeah, Maisie, she'd be happy we found each other."

EPILOGUE

"**H**ang on!" Maisie yelled from the fence line as the horse bucked like a wild animal with Hayes on its back. This time, he wore a helmet and a protective riding vest that she'd seen bull riders wear. "Oh my God, he's going to kill himself."

Beckett snorted a laugh. "Hell no. He was forced to stay away from the farm because of the last fall. He'll stick this time, believe me."

Maisie could barely look. She peeked through her fingers, scared to death Hayes was going to get thrown off. But then she realized Beckett was right. Hayes leaned back and held the reins tight so the horse couldn't buck him. The moment the horse realized Hayes wasn't coming off, the horse stopped and snorted, sounding like a pissed-off man throwing a giant temper tantrum.

She kept quiet, silently watching Hayes work, and it was the most beautiful thing she'd ever witnessed. The connection between horse and man was there—in every way Hayes moved and the way the horse responded. It wasn't all easy. The horse reared a few times, bucked in attitude, but Hayes was firm yet understanding. He let the horse make mistakes and rewarded him when he got things right.

Maisie knew why he needed this. It all suddenly made sense. Hayes understood what it felt like to be broken. Working at the farm gave him a way to fix the brokenness in these horses. On the verge of tears, she forced herself to think of something else. They were happy. They were engaged. No more sadness. They'd done enough of that. This was their time.

When Hayes finally had the horse walking around the ring slow and easy, the horse covered in sweat, he stopped in the middle of the ring and dismounted. He removed his safety gear, untacked the horse and walked away, the horse watching him like even he didn't know what in the hell had happened. He had obviously planned to kill the human on his back, and somehow that human's touch shifted his entire world until trust was formed. Yeah, Maisie got that. Hayes had magical hands.

"Not a bad start," said Hayes, opening the gate to join her and Beckett outside the sand ring.

Maisie snorted. "You make it sound like that was easy."

"Last time he got a jump on me and I lost my balance," Hayes said, clearing his throat. "That won't happen again."

Maisie nudged him with her shoulder. "Or maybe he was just helping by putting you in my path for a road trip."

Hayes grinned and dropped his head, until his lips were near hers. "Should I thank him then for wanting to kill me?"

"No thanks needed, but maybe be a little more understanding." She pressed her breasts against his warm chest.

"I'll take that into consideration." Then he dropped his mouth and kissed her until they were both breathing deep.

Beckett heaved a long sigh. "I am here with you, you know."

Hayes leaned away, giving Beckett a shit-eating grin, and reached for him. "Come here, bud. I'll give you a kiss too."

Beckett responded with a hard punch to the shoulder, sending the men into laughter.

Maisie shook her head at them and reached into her pocket as her cell rang. She looked the screen. "Hi, Clara," she answered.

"I need you. Come home."

Clara never needed anyone or anything, and the tremble in her voice sent a cold blade of ice into Maisie's gut. "What's happened?"

"I can't explain over the phone. Just come home. Alone."

The line went dead. Maisie stared at the phone, a thousand questions swirling in her mind.

Hayes's strong hand slid along her back. "Is everything okay?"

"I don't know." She looked up at him. "I need to go home. Something's happened. Clara's upset."

Hayes handed Beckett the tack. "I'll come with you."

"No," Maisie countered, pressing a hand against his strong, damp chest. "She wants me alone. I'll call you soon. Promise." She pressed a quick kiss to his lips and ran to her MINI.

The drive home should have taken twenty minutes. She got there in eleven. Once she reached the house, she threw the car into park and ran up the porch steps into the house. Mason was nowhere in sight, but she found Amelia and Clara sitting around the kitchen table. Three glasses of scotch already there. Uh-oh. Scotch always meant trouble. "What's happened?" Maisie asked, scared to move.

Clara finally lifted her head, her skin ashen. "It's Sullivan."

Maisie exchanged a long look with Amelia, who

shrugged. Sullivan Keene was Clara's one true love. They'd had a passionate romance during college. Everyone thought they'd get married. Until he moved to New York City to be a professional baseball player, leaving Clara brokenhearted at home. "What about Sullivan?"

Clara visibly swallowed. "Today, as you know, I went to the distributor who showed interest in Foxy Diva."

"Yes," Maisie said.

"Sullivan was there," Clara barely whispered. "He's stepped back from baseball for a bit, I guess, and his uncle owns the distribution company. He's been there helping out."

"Okay," Maisie said, taking a seat across from Clara. "Got it."

Clara stared down into her scotch glass, slowly shaking her head. "This is bad. So bad."

Maisie exchanged a long look with Amelia, who turned to Clara and said, "You're going to have to fill in the missing pieces. I'm not really getting why this is bad enough to make you look like you've seen a ghost."

Clara reached for her glass of scotch and downed the entire thing in one gulp. She slammed the glass down and wiped her mouth, very unladylike. Very unlike Clara. "His uncle is sending him to check out the brewery."

Maisie tried to piece things together. "Which is bad because you're still hurt, and you don't want to see him again?"

"No." Clara shook her head, adamant. When she looked between the sisters, she took a deep, pained breath and closed her eyes. "It's not that I don't want to see him. It's *who* I don't want *him* to see."

Amelia's eyes widened.

Maisie now understood. Every suspicion Maisie and

Amelia ever had made sense, especially because Mason had a killer arm and seemed to have natural talent at baseball. "Because Sullivan is Mason's father?"

Clara stole Maisie's glass and downed that one too. "Yup, and he's coming here tomorrow to take a look at the brewery, having no idea that he's about to meet the kid he never knew about."

Maisie parted her lips and shut them, having no words.

Amelia finally sighed, pushing her glass over to Clara. "Here, you need this one too."

Clara reached for the glass as a low voice said from the doorway, "Good thing I brought the big guns."

Maisie glanced at Hayes, finding him holding a few bottles of wine and double chocolate ice cream. Her heart melted. She jumped up and met him with a hug. "I think you just got hotter. Thank for you bringing this."

He winked. "It's about time someone else took care of everyone around here."

She smiled, and her heart warmed further when Hayes said to Clara, "I heard nothing. I saw nothing. Just drink and worry about it all tomorrow."

Clara gave him a small smile and then gestured across from her, to the spot where Pops used to sit, "Well, are you just going to stand there or get drunk with us?"

Hayes's gaze locked on Maisie as he took a seat, and Maisie smiled after him. Death had caused them to have terrible, heartbreaking gatherings at this table. Life brought them ecstatic moments here. But as Maisie slid onto Hayes's lap, and he locked his arm around her, she knew these sweet, happy, middle parts mattered the most.

Don't miss Stacey Kennedy's next book in the Three Chicks Brewery series:
FEISTY RED

From USA Today bestselling author Stacey Kennedy comes a second-chance romance featuring a cowboy hero who needs some serious redeeming, a serious heroine who needs some cowboy lovin', and a mischievous little boy who needs his parents to find their happily-ever-after.

She's prepared for anything... except for the second chance with her cowboy ex she never saw coming.

Clara Carter is the brains behind Three Chicks Brewery. The oldest and most responsible of the Carter sisters, she doesn't have time for anything but taking care of her son and making sure her family's top beer, Foxy Diva, gets into bars across North America. Which means getting the brew in front of Colorado's biggest beer distributor. Unfortunately, that becomes tricky when the man in charge of distribution is none other than Sullivan Kenne, the cowboy who ran out on her seven years ago.

Sullivan's life has been one wrong move after another. First, he tried to prove himself to his bastard father by signing a contract to play professional baseball, a choice Sullivan still regrets. Then he bailed on Clara, the only woman he's ever loved. Seeing her again makes Sullivan determined to right his wrongs. Unfortunately, he wasn't counting on one of those wrongs being a six-year-old son he never knew about.

Reuniting with Clara and meeting his son is a shocking—and amazing—experience. But as much as Sullivan tries to return to his roots and be the stand-up cowboy of Clara's dreams, the reality is, she's having trouble trusting him. Luckily, Sullivan knows the way to Clara's heart, and he'll prove to her that a second chance with a cowboy is worth the risk.

Don't miss a new release or sale! Subscribe to Stacey's Mailing List.

www.staceykennedy.com/newsletter

**CHECK OUT THE NEXT BOOK IN THE
THREE CHICKS BREWERY SERIES:**

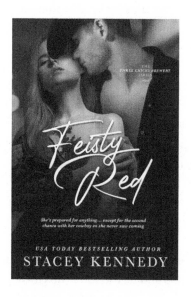

From USA Today bestselling author Stacey Kennedy
comes a second-chance romance featuring a cowboy hero
who needs some serious redeeming, a serious heroine
who needs some cowboy lovin', and a mischievous little

boy who needs his parents to find their happily-ever-after.

She's prepared for anything... except for the second chance with her cowboy ex she never saw coming.

Clara Carter is the brains behind Three Chicks Brewery. The oldest and most responsible of the Carter sisters, she doesn't have time for anything but taking care of her son and making sure her family's top beer, Foxy Diva, gets into bars across North America. Whic h means getting the brew in front of Colorado's biggest beer distributor. Unfortunately, that becomes tricky when the man in charge of distribution is none other than Sullivan Kenne, the cowboy who ran out on her seven years ago.

Sullivan's life has been one wrong move after another. First, he tried to prove himself to his bastard father by signing a contract to play professional baseball, a choice Sullivan still regrets. Then he bailed on Clara, the only woman he's ever loved. Seeing her again makes Sullivan determined to right his wrongs. Unfortunately, he wasn't counting on one of those wrongs being a six-year-old son he never knew about.

Reuniting with Clara and meeting his son is a shocking-- and amazing--experience. But as much as Sullivan tries to return to his roots and be the stand-up cowboy of Clara's dreams, the reality is, she's having trouble trusting him. Luckily, Sullivan knows the way to Clara's heart, and he'll prove to her that a second chance with a cowboy is worth the risk.

ABOUT THE AUTHOR

Stacey Kennedy is a *USA Today* bestselling author who writes contemporary romances full of heat, heart, and happily ever afters. With over 50 titles published, her books have hit Amazon, B&N, and Apple Books bestseller lists.

Stacey lives with her husband and two children in southwestern Ontario—in a city that's just as charming as any of the small towns she creates. Most days, you'll find her enjoying the outdoors with her family or venturing into the forest with her horse, Priya. Stacey's just as happy curled up indoors, where she writes surrounded by her lazy dogs. She believes that sexy books about hot cowboys or alpha heroes can fix any bad day. But wine and chocolate help too.

ACKNOWLEDGMENTS

To my husband, my children, family, friends, and bestie, it's easy to write about love when there is so much love around me. Big thanks to my readers for your friendship and your support; my editor, Lexi, for believing in me and making my stories shine; my agent, Jessica, for always having my back; the kick-ass authors in my sprint group for their endless advice and support. Thank you.

WANT TO SPEND MORE TIME IN RIVER ROCK? CHECK OUT THE FIRST BOOK IN STACEY KENNEDY'S KINKY SPURS SERIES:

DIRTY-TALKING COWBOY

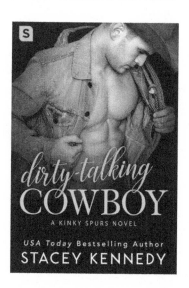

PROLOGUE

Come to Kinky Spurs, where cowboys wrangle women's hearts . . . and rope their bodies!

Emma Monroe could picture the tagline on the poster now, even the photographs of the half-naked cowboys standing by the fence, and all the other little pieces coming together to pull off a killer campaign.

Or she could, if she'd been hired as Kinky Spurs' Executive Creative Director.

Like a splash of cold water in the face, reality slammed into her as she shoved her hand into the beer cooler, grabbing the dark-brown bottle for the customer waiting at the bar. Her marketing days were long behind her now. With the frigid water dripping off her hand, the noise surrounding her in the bar returned to her. Voices created a hum through the crowd by the bar, while the country music band entertained the crowd on the dance floor with a Little Big Town cover song.

The bar was nestled in the heart of River Rock, Colorado, with the space being basically a large rectangle bookended by two stages. One for the country music band, the other for the mechanical bull and the mats surrounding it, with tables spread out between the two stages. From floor to ceiling, wood paneling set the western theme. Behind the bar was a bright-pink neon KINKY SPURS sign, large deer antlers overtop, with a shiny, reclaimed wooden slab for the bar and metal stools in front. Between the nut shells on the floor, the cowboy hats atop the heads, and the cowboy boots stomping on the dance floor in rhythm to the song, the bar couldn't get more rustic. The greasy aroma coming from the kitchen simply added to Kinky Spurs' charm.

Emma cracked open the beer in her hand, offering the bottle to the pretty blonde waiting at the bar. Blondie didn't even notice Emma, smiling sensually at the cute guy next to her. "That'll be four dollars," Emma announced, placing her beer down in front of her.

Blondie didn't even look Emma's way when she handed Emma a twenty-dollar bill. Emma laughed softly, snatched up the bill, quickly grabbing change from the register, and placed the bills and change onto the bar, still being ignored.

The band suddenly shifted songs, belting out a Keith Urban classic. Blondie squealed, "Oh, this song's my favorite!" She grabbed her beer, her change, and the woman standing next to her by the arm, then danced her way to the dance floor.

The man she'd been ogling followed.

Ah, the beginnings of sweet love. Or maybe a one-night stand.

Emma had neither of those options, and that was perfectly fine. Her sleepless nights were because of a man. She didn't want another. Focusing away from the tightness in her chest and onto her job, she reached for the cloth beneath the bar and set to cleaning up the spilled beer when something made her look up.

The air evaporated around her.

A man wove his way through the crowd, obviously arriving for the busy night at Kinky Spurs. He had to be a regular on Thursday nights. She'd seen that cowboy every Thursday since she'd started working there three weeks ago. Her heart rate kicked up a notch or two as he drew closer, like it had every time she'd seen him.

There was not a hint of weakness in him. This guy was all man, right down to his toned, muscular body. He wasn't fancy, sticking to a dark-brown cowboy hat, plaid button-down, worn blue jeans, and scuffed-up brown boots. He wore the look well, his clothes hugged his body in all the right places. His mouth curved as he approached, his gaze locked onto hers.

Apparently, he knew exactly what his presence did to her. And it was unreal.

He practically oozed strength and heat, making her want to forget she was at work all together. Though what held him apart from every other man in this room was the power contained in his silvery-blue eyes. The sharpness in those eyes captivated her, the awareness in their depths seemed to know all the things she wanted answers to. And the small smile teasing his mouth caused butterflies to flutter in her belly, flushing her skin red-hot. Suddenly, she became very aware that she only wore a tight, red T-shirt with KINKY SPURS written across her chest in bold white calligraphy and tiny denim shorts that barely covered her butt. The only thing that felt covered up at the moment were her feet, by her new dark-brown cowboy boots.

She forced herself not to turn into a babbling fool when he reached her. "What can I get you?" she asked, proud her voice came out steady and calm.

That half smile hadn't faded. If anything, his grin looked

more dangerous than ever. He slid onto the stool, his forearms resting on the bar, muscles cording. "I think it's about
time we stop this, don't you?"

That low voice was as seductive as it was addictive. No
man should have that voice. She gathered all her strength
and replied, "Pardon me?"

He leaned forward, focused on her. "How about we stop
pretending that we see anyone else in this bar but each
other?"

She nearly opened her mouth and agreed with what
he'd said. Hell, for three weeks, she only saw *him* every time
he came into the bar, until he left. For whatever unknown
reason, she was accurately aware of this guy in a way she'd
never been to anyone before. This *thing* between them had
caught her completely off guard, and whenever he was
around, she seemed to lose control of her mind.

Though on the flip side, she also got asked out at least
three times a night. She wasn't only led by her hormones.
Rules were rules. "I'm flattered, truly, and thank you, but
we're not allowed to date customers." Okay, that was a total
lie. Megan Harrison, the owner of Kinky Spurs, didn't put
those kinds of restrictions on her employees, but Emma had
learned these past weeks that her answer worked the best to
get a man's attention focusing elsewhere.

Sexy Eyes needed to look elsewhere or she'd end up in
his bed; a fact she knew with total certainty. She didn't have
the energy for a relationship, and her heart was still healing.
She was a month out of having her heart pulverized by Jake
Cadwell. Getting into any type of a relationship, even if
simply a sexual one, wasn't on her agenda tonight, or any
night for that matter. Sometimes a girl needed to breathe
without the distraction of a man.

This was her time to breathe.

Not giving Sexy Eyes the chance to talk again and pull her under a spell she'd never recover from, she turned to the woman sitting next to him. "What can I get ya?" she asked.

Sexy Eyes's answering low chuckle told Emma he wasn't anywhere near done with her yet.

"Rum and Coke," the brunette replied.

Emma grabbed a glass from the bar, fighting against the shaking of her hand when she reached for the bottle of rum. *Dammit.* Sexy Eyes had been in her thoughts all the time, especially late at night. And that had been without ever talking to him. If he added charm into this obvious chemistry between them, she wouldn't say no to him. And she needed to say no. Or at least her heart needed to say no.

When she added the Coke from the soda gun, her gaze lifted to the spot Sexy Eyes had been, and he was gone. Emma blew out a long breath, forcing the flutters in her belly to calm.

"I need to call in a favor tonight."

Emma blinked and glanced sideways, finding Megan sidling up next to her. With her trim figure, freckles dusting her nose, wavy sandy-brown hair, and her unique eyes—one a crystal blue and the other a warm brown—she stood out in the crowd, for sure. Everything about Megan screamed strength and sensuality, and as the owner of Kinky Spurs at only twenty-eight years old, she clearly had a good head on her shoulders. "What favor?" Emma asked.

Megan reached for the microphone next to the cash register. "You don't have any objection in taking part in *Rope 'Em Up,* do you?"

"Depends on what the game is." Emma had seen some of the games that happened at Kinky Spurs every Thursday, Friday, and Saturday night at ten o'clock. Last week, four women willingly let themselves be hog-tied by four cowboys. The winner received a free dinner at the bar. Emma didn't think that was enough of a reward.

"It's nothing crazy." Megan smiled, probably at the trepidation crossing Emma's face. "You'll be a horse."

Emma blinked. "I'll be a horse?"

"Yup." Megan nodded. "You'll get roped, then your wrists will be tied. No big deal."

Emma's lips parted to refuse her. She closed them immediately after and reconsidered. Last week, another bartender volunteered and went up on stage. That seemed to only happen when Megan didn't have enough women to take part in the games. She finally sighed. "Well, I suppose it's my turn to take one for the team, isn't it?"

Megan patted Emma on the arm. "You're a doll. I owe you."

The bar seemed to get a whole lot smaller as Megan weaved her way through the crowd toward the stage. For the most part, people who came to Kinky Spurs were here for their famous chicken wings that went from mild to sweat-your-ass-off hot, and for the local craft beer. Except for Thursday, Friday, and Saturday nights. Those nights belonged to the students from the nearby University of Colorado, the twenty-somethings that lived in River Rock, as well as the tourists, who wanted a little something *extra* than a typical night out at the club.

From what Emma had learned since she began working there, the bar had originally been owned by Gerald Kinky. When Megan had bought the place two years ago after Gerald retired, she'd been inspired by the bar's name and decided to hold a kinky game that was sex related to draw in a fun crowd. Of course, Megan didn't allow sexual intercourse to happen in her bar, but she was smart enough to know sex sells. And apparently at Kinky Spurs it sold, since for the three weeks that Emma had been there, the place had been packed.

When Megan finally reached the stage, standing by the mechanical bull, she waved Emma forward. Ducking under the bar, Emma made it onto the stage just as Megan lifted the microphone to her mouth. "We all know why you came to the Spurs, and it wasn't just for the beer and our famous chicken wings . . ." she announced. "*Rope 'Em Up* is about to begin." The crowd went wild, inching their way closer to the stage until they all gathered in front of Megan. She lifted her hand, quieting them down before she continued, "Will the contestants please join me on stage?"

Emma's cheeks began to burn almost as if she had a low-grade fever, but the heat wasn't due to sickness or because of the three couples joining her on stage. The feverish sweat forming along her flesh was because Sexy Eyes had jumped onto the stage. Each step he took toward her seemed to make the air thicker, charged by something so powerful that she couldn't control. Those captivating eyes were on her, that killer smile back, warming her in places she simply shouldn't be heating up in front of an audience.

He stopped a few feet away from her and grabbed the rope on the stage waiting for him. When his head lifted again, he winked. *Dear Lord.* Emma almost reached for the hem of her panties to make sure they stayed in place.

Before she could get a handle on herself, Megan called, "Cowboys, rope your ladies."

Everything right then and there melted away. All she saw was *him*, and the cowboy's hands working the rope expertly into a lasso. There was something uniquely sensual about the way he handled the rope. Would he handle her body with the same careful regard? God, she wanted to find out. Her heart skipped a beat or two when his eyes lifted to hers again, and that half smile weakened her knees. That's when his brows furrowed, his wise eyes narrowing on his target. Her.

Not a second later, he tossed the rope in her direction. She gasped as the soft rope slid oh-so-perfectly along her bare arms. Another gasp ripped from her throat when he jerked the rope, causing the lasso to tighten. Something changed in his expression then. Something that pulled them together with uncontrollable force.

He approached with long, unhurried strides, tugging her forward at the same time. She seemed to get closer to him in the blink of an eye. In that instant, she became a woman she didn't recognize. A woman who hungered for a man so intensely that she was aware of his every move, every breath, and hell, even the strength he seemed to project out into the world.

She had one second to stare into the heat in his eyes before he used the rope to spin her around. His spicy, woodsy cologne whirled around her, and it was all she could do to fight against the desire to press herself against the hard planes of his tall, muscular physique.

"Put your wrists together for me, sweetheart," he murmured, slow and unhurried, as if he had all the time in the world.

She shivered and obliged him. Not once had he touched her, and she wondered if that was because he was a gentleman or because he didn't trust himself, in the same way she currently didn't trust herself.

One loop slid over her left wrist, and her eyes fluttered shut as heat flooded her, a foreign sense of desire swelling inside. When another loop drifted over her right wrist, warmth pooled in her belly, slowly growing hotter each time he tightened the rope. Her chest lifted and fell quickly, and as he stroked the inside of her wrist, an uncontrollable moan spilled from her mouth.

His low chuckle sizzled over her. "What's your name, darlin'?" he asked.

Her breath hitched and she trembled, knowing he'd likely heard and felt both. "Emma," she replied.

"Well, Emma, I'm Shep Blackshaw, and you better stop doing what you're doing." His voice lowered, thick and rumbly, as he stepped a little closer, pressing his erection against her bottom. "Or I'm about to do something very inappropriate in front of a crowd."

Surely that warning should've broken the spell he cast over her. It didn't. The low tenor of his voice held promise of a night she'd never forget. Instead of answering him, and on total instinct, she shivered again, as his startling power washed over her.

Desperate not to make a complete ass out of herself on the third week of her new job, she stared straight ahead, afraid if she opened her mouth, she'd beg him to touch her right in front of everyone. He finished the binding and gave a final tug, showing her how locked in she was. He held the rope between the cuffs he'd made as if he owned her.

She couldn't move, couldn't breathe. From head to toe, she flushed with an unnatural heat, her limbs trembled with need, begging him to make this game real. His finger slid along the inside of her wrist, and again, a moan broke free.

Oh, how that touch would feel sliding between her thighs. She pressed herself against his cock and wiggled a little bit, inviting him to do whatever he wanted.

His warm breath tickled her ear when he groaned. "No matter how tempting it is to keep you like this a little longer and make you moan a bit louder, I don't like to lose." Coldness spilled over her as his hands were gone. He threw them up in the air, declaring himself the winner.

Thunderous applause from the crowd broke the spell that he'd put her under. She snapped her eyes open, staring ahead at the drum set. Her panties were drenched.

In those seconds of reprieve without his touch, she inhaled and exhaled repeatedly, until her body and mind belonged to her again. When he began untying her, she felt more stable on her feet, the heat simmering on the surface instead of boiling over. Only then did she dare turn around, refusing to meet his eyes, fearful he'd see how turned on she was.

By the bar, behind the crowd gathered before the stage, she noticed one of the blonde bartenders and her new friend, Harper McKinney, fanning herself with a piece of paper. She mouthed the word, *wow*. Before Emma had a chance to respond, a firm finger pressed under her chin, lifting her gaze to meet silvery-blue power beneath his brown cowboy hat.

A smile teased Shep's sculpted lips. "So, Emma, after that little show you just gave me," he said, letting the rope hang from his hand like a promise he planned to keep. "I think there's really only one thing that needs to be asked now, don't you?"

"What's that?" she barely managed.

He leaned in closer, bringing all that heat and man within centimeters of her, and he arched a single eyebrow. "Your place or mine?"

Made in the USA
Monee, IL
24 July 2020

36944528R00142